# Highland Fling

## A Ransom & Fortune Adventure
## Volume 1

## Michelle Miles

Highland Fling: A Ransom and Fortune Adventure

Book Cover by Erin Dameron-Hill

First Edition: February 19, 2019

ISBN: 9781540197252 (eBook)
ISBN: 9781734306835 (paperback)

# Chapter One
## The Time Bender

DANE FORTUNE PULLED HIS vehicle into the parking lot of Goldenrod Research Technology and parked. He leaned back in the leather seat, gazing up at the four-story glass and metal building wondering why the CEO, William Ransom, felt the need to hire him. All he knew about the company was they developed new technology for computer companies.

What was so dangerous about that?

He knew even less about the CEO other than what he'd read on the company website. William Ransom was former military with a genius level IQ and an almost mad-scientist persona. According to his bio, he was married, had one child and liked to garden in his spare time. He lived in a million-dollar house in the suburbs of Arlington, Virginia, not far from where GRT, as it was called, was located.

Dane exited the car and headed into the building where he was met by two security guards behind a long desk. A computer screen with *Welcome! To begin, tap here* and the company logo faced him. He was greeted with icy stares and a chilly reception from both of them.

"I'm here to see Mr. Ransom."

One of the guards stood and pointed to the screen. "Please sign in with your name and contact information."

Dane blinked. "Why do you need contact information?"

"Do you have an appointment?" the guard asked, his tone clipped.

"Yes."

"Sign in and I will alert his assistant."

It didn't escape him the guard refused to answer his question.

With a shake of his head, Dane used his forefinger to type in his name and phone number, the date and the time of his appointment. The security guard handed him a visitor badge, then motioned to the small seating area in the lobby.

"You can wait there."

Dismissed, Dane moved to the ultra-contemporary chairs and had just sat when a woman exited the elevator and headed toward him. The only sound was that of her heels clicking on the tile floor. She was dressed in a smart business suit—straight skirt, jacket and white shirt. Her dark hair was pulled up into a tight bun at the back of her head. She smiled as she approached.

"You must be Mr. Fortune. I'm Louise, William's assistant." She extended her hand as he got to his feet.

He shook her hand. "Nice to meet you."

"If you'll follow me." She waved to the elevators. "He's expecting you."

The security guards eyed him as he followed the woman to the elevator. They rode up to the fourth floor in silence. At the glass doors, she used her badge to gain entry and then turned left down a long hallway.

The office space was decorated in monochromatic colors. White walls. Gray cubes. Grayer carpet. They passed a group of cubicles heading to the wall of offices at the back. She halted at the one in the corner, gave a brief knock and announced him. She motioned Dane inside.

The corner office was huge. The desk was centered in the room with a conference table big enough for twelve on one side and a small conversation area on the other with a sofa, loveseat, two chairs, and a glass and metal coffee table in the center.

"Could I get you water or coffee?"

Dane shook his head. "No, thanks."

As he entered the large corner office, a man with salt-and-pepper hair rounded the desk to greet him. He wore slacks and a white button-down shirt with the sleeves rolled up to the elbows.

"Dane Fortune, nice to meet you."

Louise closed the door behind her as she exited. William punched a button on a remote and the electric shades descended, blocking out the morning sun and view of the employee parking lot behind the building. Beyond the lot, a greenbelt.

"Thank you for coming on such short notice, Mr. Fortune."

"It's Dane. What can I do for you, sir?" He lowered into one of the chairs, lacing his fingers and leaning his forearms on his knees.

"Please call me William. I intend for our working relationship to be a close one and, God willing, long term." He poured a cup of coffee, added cream and sugar, and then took the seat opposite him. He took a sip. "Do you have any idea what the company does?"

"Not much. Something about computers."

He smiled. "Yes, we've helped develop new faster processors for computers such as Dell and HP. The gaming industry is very interested in our virtual reality developments as well." He paused, took another sip. "But we also have government contracts. Most of the technology we develop for them is top secret and requires top secret clearance to work on the projects. NASA and DARPA are particularly interested in our work here."

A sudden tingling sensation prickled the back of his neck. He understood, then, why William Ransom might feel like his life was in jeopardy if his company was working with an agency like DARPA.

"I used to be a military man myself before I entered the private sector," he continued, sounding as though he was reminiscing about the past. "I turned down a lucrative opportunity with the Department of Defense, but it seems once they realize what you can do, they don't want to let you go." He gave a stiff smile.

Dane's brows drew together. Where was he going with this?

"The company is a federally funded research and development center. With DARPA, we're committed to creating major breakthroughs for national security," William continued. "We also worked with NASA on their latest manned mission to Mars. You may have heard about that in the news."

Dane nodded as he leaned back in his chair. He dropped his foot to the floor. "I did hear about that. Is that why you want to hire me as part of your executive protection team?"

"You *are* the executive protection team, Dane." He grinned again before taking another sip of coffee, then placed the cup on the glass table in front of him.

"You mean you don't have anyone else on the team?"

"Not yet, no. But it's come to my attention I'm in need of protection. As is my wife and daughter. I've received death threats." William rose and walked across the room to his desk. He rummaged through a drawer, pulled out a folder and walked back to Dane, handing it to him.

Dane took the folder, flipped it open. He was faced with letter after letter threatening not only William's life but his family's. Ugly death threats with details of specific things this person wanted to do to the wife and daughter before killing them and then killing William. His stomach knotted into a tight fist as he looked up at the man who sat calmly across from him.

"How long has this been going on?" Dane asked.

"Two weeks. It started with one letter I received here, then quickly escalated. I've been getting them at the house. It's been difficult to keep my wife from seeing them. Yesterday, a decapitated cat appeared on the front doorstep."

"I'm beginning to understand why you need protection." Dane flipped the folder closed. He dropped it on the table.

William nodded agreement. "This is a job working directly for me. All you have to do is name your price."

"My security company charges—"

"No." He shook his head. "You misunderstand. Not your security company. You."

Dane stared at him for a long moment. "Are you asking for around the clock protection for the three of you?"

"Yes."

He shook his head. "I need a team for that. At least five guys who are trained for something like that."

"Like you?" William sat back in the sofa. "I read your file."

Dane cocked his head to one side. "My file?"

"Former Army Ranger with a stint in the Secret Service. You left when you failed to protect the First Lady during the assassination attempt on President Kunkle's life. You blame yourself for her death when in reality you were the only reason the president and his teenage son are alive today. You joined Peregrine Protection Agency three years ago as a consultant in security for high-level executives. You've consulted on jobs in all industries, from oil and gas to engineering to banking."

Dane clenched his jaw. He hadn't fully grasped how resourceful William Ransom was. If he knew that much about his work life, what did he know about his personal life? "Did you enjoy digging into my past?"

"No. It's not something I enjoy. But it was necessary. I have many friends still in the military and the Department of Defense as well as the Secret Service. You were the best at what you did and came highly recommended," William said. "And that's why I want to hire you."

Dane took a deep breath, exhaled it. "It's a job bigger than one person."

"It is." He nodded agreement. "But I can't have more than one person on the job. My wife is...fragile. She's battling a rare form of bladder cancer. I don't need her upset. It's why I've been developing a new technology. And it's also why I believe I've been receiving death threats."

"What is this new technology?"

"It's groundbreaking, really." William reached for his coffee, took a sip. "To tell you that, I'll need you to sign a non-disclosure agreement. I can't give you the NDA unless you agree to work for me."

So that was the deal, then. In order to get to the bottom of the whole death threat thing, Dane was going to have to agree. He was still convinced the job required a security detail of at least five, especially with the horrid threats he'd seen in the folder.

"So, Mr. Fortune, do you agree?"

He considered as he looked at William who calmly sat across from him, waiting for an answer. Dane didn't want to say no because he knew the man really did need the protection, as did his family. And he was never one to say no to someone like him who was in desperate need.

"I agree." He'd insist on hiring four more men once they got all the details confirmed.

William placed his cup on the table, rose and left the office. A moment later, he returned with a two-page document requiring his signature and his promise that he wouldn't speak of this new technology outside this room. He scribbled his name on the signature line and dated it. William signed next to his. The man sat back in the cushions of the sofa and took a deep breath.

"I've developed a time machine," William said.

Dane stared at him in disbelief. "A time machine?"

He nodded. "Yes. Fully functional, too. I've spent the last eight months working on it with a small team made up of people I trust completely."

"And...you developed this to help your wife how?"

"By going forward in time to the future. My hope is that the advances in medicine will have found a cure for her cancer."

The man was out of his mind. How could he think taking his wife to the future would cure her? There was no guarantee it would work, much less there *was* a cure for it in the future.

"You said you had a team you trusted. Are you sure everyone on that team is someone you can trust?" Dane asked.

William's brows knit. "I don't follow."

"Do you think someone on that team is responsible for the death threats?"

He gave a sharp shake of his head. "Not possible. Conner Dade has been with me for years and has been on the team since I came up with the idea. He was instrumental in helping to create the technology. Thomas Hardy is one of my best computer guys and has figured out a way to integrate the time machine into an operating system to help track it. Lucy Wakefield is a theoretical physicist whose work on the space-time continuum is why I picked her and why I've gotten this far."

"Just the three of them, then?" he asked.

"Yes. None of them would betray me."

He sounded so certain, Dane almost believed him. But he'd been around long enough and knew people well enough to know there was always more to the story. Someone close to William Ransom was the one sending the death threats or had hired someone to send the death threats. The bottom line was someone wanted William out of the way to get their hands on this new technology.

"What does this time machine look like?"

He broke into a broad grin and rose, walking back to his desk. He picked up another folder and carried it back, handing it to Dane. "It's genius, actually. No bigger than the size of a lipstick. It has a readout to show the destination date and one small button to transport the user to that destination. I call it the time bender."

Dane looked at the schematic of the small time bender and then a rendering of the thing. "You've already built this?"

"I have a prototype," he said with a nod.

Dane flipped the folder closed. He'd seen and heard enough. He knew he had his work cut out for him. "Then let's get started with your security detail."

# Chapter Two
## Hitman

ARCHIMEDES "ARK" CRANE CROUCHED at the window in the abandoned building, peering across the street at Third Street Café in downtown Arlington watching Emily Ransom. She sat at one of the tables on the patio sipping sparkling water and reading a paperback.

When Ark found out she was suffering from cancer, it made his decision to accept the job harder than usual. He didn't like killing women. He especially didn't like killing a woman like Emily. For all he knew, she had several more years, even if her cancer hadn't riddled her body. But for the moment, she seemed well enough to take herself out to lunch.

He was a sniper once. One of the best. He angled the gun and looked through the scope, getting her in his sights. It was only a matter of when he'd pull the trigger. Not if.

As his finger hovered over the trigger, a white van screeched down the street toward the café. Ark straightened and watched. It didn't appear to be slowing down as it hit the sidewalk seating and then crashed through the glass windows of the café. Tables and people went flying.

Three guys got out of the van wielding guns and firing at anyone who moved as they hurried past injured patrons and into the café.

Ark abandoned his post in the empty building, ran down the stairs to the first floor and then across the street. The noise had drawn a crowd of people who stood in the street and gawked, trying to decide what to do. He pulled out his hand gun, shouting at the people on the street to stay back and call the police.

He hurried past the abandoned van and found his way inside to the three gunmen. They were in the kitchen threatening a man who appeared to be the manager. The staff was huddled in a corner, trying to stay out of the line of fire, fear on all their faces.

"You owe us," the lead henchman said, holding the gun to the man's head. "Where is our money?"

"I-I don't have it."

Ark didn't care why the manager owed the guy money because it didn't matter. What mattered was he'd interrupted his hit and that was inexcusable. He took aim and fired three consecutive rounds, killing all three henchmen. The manager turned wide eyes on him, his hands raised.

"Get out of here. All of you," Ark said.

"Are you police?" the manager asked.

"No, but they're on their way."

The manager and his four workers scurried out of the kitchen toward the back. Likely to exit through a back door.

Ark headed back through the wreckage of the café to find Emily Ransom. She was on the ground by a toppled table. Her head was bleeding. A pool of crimson spread underneath her. When they exited the van, they'd started shooting and she was one of their first victims. She looked up at him, confusion etched on her face.

"What happened?" Her voice was barely above a whisper.

"You're safe now." Ark raised his gun and fired.

ARK LEFT THE GRISLY scene behind. He was oblivious to the blood on the walls and floor, the bodies littering the café. Emily Ransom was dead. It couldn't have been executed more beautifully. He wasn't sure why the manager was in trouble with the henchmen—perhaps he owed a lot of money to a loan shark—but he was glad it gave him the perfect coverup to his hit of Emily Ransom.

He strode out through the kitchen of the café, stepping over more dead bodies. Out the back door, he walked two blocks and slid into the leather seat of his posh sports car. He reached for the briefcase Conner Dade had given him a few hours before and opened the thick manila folder.

It could have been an FBI case file, it was so well put together. Everything the man knew about William and Emily Ransom was there. When they got up, when they slept, when and where they ate. Even when they made love, for God's sake.

He had two more hits to complete——William Ransom and his daughter, Skye. He glanced at his watch. Ark knew he could find William at his office. He was counting on that.

When that job was complete, he'd take care of the daughter.

SKYE RANSOM JOGGED DOWN the sidewalk then ran up the stairs to her apartment, the music blaring in her ears. She always started the day with a morning jog before heading to class at Georgetown University.

She unlocked her door and flung it open, yanking the earphones off her head.

Coffee and a shower were her next order of business. She liked the TV on for background noise as she got ready for school. She flipped it on and tossed the remote on the sofa, then headed to the kitchen. As she waited for her one-cup coffeemaker to brew her a cup, she heard the breaking news interrupt the regular program.

"We have breaking news coming out of downtown Arlington," the female news anchor announced, glancing down at a page in front of her. "Third Street Café was hit by a runaway van this afternoon during the lunch crowd. It's unclear the motives of the driver. Witnesses report seeing the van crash through the patio seating. Three armed men then got out and started shooting."

Skye spun around, staring at the television. She knew that was her parents' favorite lunchtime restaurant. Her heart kicked into high gear as she watched the news report showing the wreckage of the café. She pressed her white-knuckled fist against her mouth. Yellow crime scene tape was wrapped around the building.

"Forty-one victims, including restaurant staff, were found dead inside," she reported. "Three armed gunmen wearing black ski masks were also found dead on the scene. Police are speculating the hit might have been part of a bizarre murder-suicide pact. They aren't ruling out that other perpetrators may be involved. We'll go live now to our reporter at the café..."

Skye tuned out the rest of the report as she snatched her cell phone, quickly dialing her father. There was no answer. She tried her mother. When there was still no answer, her breath quickened, and her heart pounded.

*Tell me they weren't there today,* she thought. *Tell me they've both forgotten to turn on their cell phones. Tell me I'm over-reacting.*

Fear knotted in her stomach. Her coffee and classes forgotten, she grabbed her car keys off the counter and dashed for the door.

HER CELL PHONE RANG as she raced for her father's office. Skye's heart leapt into her throat. She glanced down and saw her caller ID blinking her father's name. *Thank God!* Grasping the steering wheel with one hand, she snatched her phone with the other.

"Dad! Are you all right?"

"Of course, I am. Why wouldn't I be?" Her father sounded bewildered.

"Didn't you hear?" The light at the intersection she approached changed to yellow. She floored it, running through to a chorus of honks. "Where's Mom? Is she with you?"

"She's at home, or should be," he replied.

At his words, her heart sank to her toes. Her mother had never not taken her call or called her right back.

"Skye, what's wrong? Is everything all right?"

"No, everything is not all right. Something happened," she whispered, a lump in her throat. "Something terrible."

"What's that? You're breaking up, Skye. I can't hear you."

"Stay there. I'm coming to you." She hung up.

ARK CRANE BACKED HIS vehicle into a secluded spot beneath a low-hanging tree. He'd maneuvered his car to the greenbelt on the other side of the employee parking lot to set up his next job. The building in front of him was host to a wall of windows and William Ransom's office in the corner. With his laptop perched in the center of the front seat, he opened it, put in his earpiece and started listening. He'd bugged the man's office days ago.

Ark knew Ransom had been receiving death threats—he'd been the one sending them after all—so he knew what the six-foot-two dark haired man was doing there. Ark had cloned William's phone and knew he'd been looking for security protection.

This guy he'd hired didn't seem all that badass. As soon as his name was announced, Ark started searching for everything he could find on Dane Fortune. Sure, he was a former Army Ranger. Sure, he'd been in the Secret Service. But that didn't mean much to Ark. He, himself, was former Navy SEAL. They'd be evenly matched in a fight. And wouldn't that be fun?

Ark picked up his phone and made a call.

"Conner Dade," answered his current employer.

"I'm here. Send me the feed," Ark said and hung up. A man of few words, he preferred to keep the conversation light.

He waited, watching the cursor until it blinked *connected*. Conner Dade was William Ransom's employee, one of his most trusted, in fact. That Conner was pulling a feat of murderous treason worthy of a Shakespearean play made no difference one way or the other to Ark. All that mattered was that he'd been paid to do a job.

He was now hooked into the building's security system. He had access to every camera and easily found Ransom's corner office on the fourth floor. His assistant sat in an open cube outside his door. Behind her, a large section of cubicles was mostly empty. Ark knew by the floor plan that area of the building was reserved for the executives. The lab was a couple of floors below the first level with some of the highest security he'd ever seen. Everyone had to be scanned to go through security. They were required to surrender their cell phones upon entry as well as verify their identity with fingerprints and retinal scans.

All that security made Ark wonder what was in that lab that was so important.

Not that he really cared. All he cared about was getting paid. Conner Dade was in a hurry to get things done. He wanted the entire Ransom family dead and out of the way and he was willing to pay a lot of money for it to be done.

Once they were all dead, he'd collect a nice sum in his offshore account and get out of the country. He'd already packed his bags and booked a flight to Belize.

Ark readied his gun and waited for the target.

Skye pulled into the parking lot of her father's building, her tires screeching. She parked and hurried inside. Impatience lanced through her as she stopped at security to check in.

"Is he expecting you?" the security guy asked.

"Cut the crap, George. I'm his daughter and you know it. This is urgent. Life or death urgent. Now give me the damn visitor badge." She waved her open hand at him.

"You still have to sign in." He motioned to the computer screen.

She groaned annoyance as she quickly tapped in her name. He extended the visitor badge to her. She snatched it out of his hand and started for the elevators.

"Skye, wait. I have to call his assistant."

"Not waiting," she called over her shoulder as she punched the elevator button.

It opened a second later and she got in, hitting the number four button over and over until the doors finally closed and she was on her way up. She hurried through the doors and down the hallway to her father's corner office. Louise saw her coming and stepped into her path.

"Skye, he's in the middle of a confidential meeting," she said.

"I don't care. He knows I'm coming. Let me by. I have to see him."

"But he's—"

"I think my mother is dead." Her voice hitched as she interrupted the woman.

Shock registered on her face as it drained of color. She stepped aside. "Go in."

Skye burst through the office door. Her father was seated on the sofa. A man she didn't know was across from him. The both looked up in surprise as she barreled into the room.

"Dad." Instantly, her eyes filled with tears.

He got to his feet. The stranger followed suit. Her father came to her, grasped her in a hug. "Skye, what is it? What's happened?"

"The café...there was a robbery or something. Everyone is dead. I couldn't get Mom on the phone."

"What café?"

"Third Street." Frustration and panic laced her words. She ran a hand over her sweat-dampened hair.

Her father looked at the man. "Find my wife." The man nodded and left the room. William put an arm around her shoulders and walked her toward the desk. "I'm sure she's fine. Come sit down. Louise, bring some water."

"I tried calling her more than once. She never answered."

Her father stood behind the desk, looking down at his cell phone. Skye knew he had an app to track her mother's phone. He'd added it when she was first diagnosed. It gave them all peace of mind to know he could find her anywhere, anytime.

Skye peered intently at her father, watching every imperceptible movement of his face. She could tell by the way he held his mouth and the way his eyes were suddenly clouded he knew where her mother was.

"She's at the café, isn't she?"

"Her phone is. That's all I know."

"Dad, the news said there were no survivors. That all were killed. That—"

Her words cut off as the window behind her father shattered in a hail of gunfire. Skye fell to the floor in front of the desk as her father dropped to the floor on the other side.

"Dad!"

Another shower of bullets as she hovered on the ground. Splinters of desk flew around her. She heard a distinct groan from her father. And then everything stopped. She jumped up and ran to him. He laid face-down, sprawled on the floor.

"Oh, no. Please no."

Her feet crunched on broken glass. A pool of blood spread under him. She choked on her tears and knelt, rolling him over. Cradling his head in her lap, Skye brushed her father's hair off his bloody forehead. She looked frantically toward the doorway.

"Help!" she screamed. "Somebody help me!"

The man returned holding a gun as he ran toward the shattered windows.

"Stay down," he ordered, then returned fire. An eerie silence fell over the office.

"Skye..." Her father gasped her name. She looked down at him, tears blurring her vision. "Time bender. Protect the...time bender."

Those were his last words as he died in her arms.

# Chapter Three
## The Package

AFTER THE FUNERALS, SKYE packed up her apartment and moved into her parent's home. She'd talked to the police numerous times about her father's suspicious death. They ruled it a random act of violence since they couldn't find any suspects. It was something Skye didn't believe at all, especially with the death of her mother the same day.

She'd tried to find the man in her father's office that was there that day. All she knew was his name was Dane Fortune. She didn't recall much about that day, nor did she remember what this Dane Fortune looked like. Louise had the name of the security company he worked for and contacted them several times. The receptionist told her the same thing every time—Mr. Fortune wasn't taking new clients and in fact was on a leave of absence.

And so, she turned her attention to more important matters. The burden of handling her parent's estate fell to her. It had become overwhelming at times, but Skye did her best to maintain her composure, her calm, her cool. She consulted with a realtor and prepared to put the four-thousand-square-foot house on the market. She wasn't exactly up for maintaining the house, nor did she need all that space as a single woman.

She'd also consulted with an art dealer and an appraiser to look at the art and antiques her father collected. She had no use for all that. What they didn't want, she'd planned to sell in an estate sale. She'd been busy culling through her parent's personal belongings the last several days. It was a dirty, thankless, lonely job. She was tired, sweaty, dusty, hungry and in need of a stiff drink. She was on day three of packing when the doorbell rang.

Wiping her dirty palms on the front of her jeans, she headed down the stairs to the front door. Through the window in the door, she could see the silhouette of a man and assumed it was either the art dealer or the antique guy. So, when she opened the door to a tall, dark-haired man with sharp blue eyes, she was surprised.

"Can I help you?"

"You must be Skye." He extended his hand.

They shook in greeting, but she didn't invite him inside. He looked vaguely familiar, but she couldn't place him. "Do I know you?"

"Dane Fortune. I briefly knew your father. Can I come in?" He motioned inside the cavernous house.

She stepped aside and allowed him into the entry way. He took a long look around at the twenty-foot vaulted ceiling, the winding staircase and the black and while classic tile flooring in the foyer. An antique table in the entry hosted an oversized vase with colorful silk flowers reaching toward the ceiling. A crystal and brushed nickel chandelier completed the entryway décor.

"Nice place."

"Mr. Fortune, I'm not trying to be rude, but I am in the middle of something and I'm expecting a few others later today, and—"

"I'll get to it, then. Your parents were murdered."

She blinked surprise as her heart skittered into a halt. "The police said—"

"They don't know shit. My guess is they were paid off to stop looking into the homicides."

"And how do you know this?" She propped her hands on her hips.

"Your father tried to hire me as his personal security detail the day he died because he'd been receiving death threats. I think a hitman took them both out."

She dropped her arms, not knowing how to respond. She looked him over again and remembered where she'd seen him. He'd been the stranger in her father's office when she burst through the door. The day her mother died. The day her father was killed. He'd told this Dane Fortune to find his wife.

This was the man she'd been looking for.

"You were the one at his office that day."

He'd returned fire to whoever it was that shot and killed her father. As her father took his last breath, Dane dashed out of the office.

He nodded. "You came in worried about your mother. After I left the office, I tried to get to her, but it was too late."

Skye knew. Her mother had been shot multiple times. Once in the head, execution style.

"You didn't know about the death threats, did you?"

She shook her head.

"He was trying to shield you and your mother from it. I guess he did a pretty good job."

She remained mute as she turned and headed to the kitchen. She needed that stiff drink sooner rather than later, even though it wasn't noon yet. It was noon somewhere. She poured a glass of bourbon, downed it, poured another one.

"Little early for drinking, isn't it?"

"My parents are dead and you're telling me they were killed by a hitman, so forgive me for wanting something to take the edge off."

She glared at him across the kitchen island, pissed he was judging her. Also pissed she looked like hell. She hadn't showered yet because she got up early that morning to start packing boxes. Her hair was pulled back into a ponytail. Sweat dampened her neck and back. She had dirt under her fingernails. Dust coated her clothes.

Skye gave him a good once-over. He was packing. She could see the small bulge of the gun under his left arm even though he tried to conceal it under his sport coat. Who the hell was this guy?

"What do you want?" she asked.

"I agreed to be your father's security detail."

He paused. She narrowed her gaze. "Yeah, so?"

"So, I intend to be your security detail now."

She snorted a laugh. "I don't need a babysitter, Mr. Whoever-You-Are."

"Fortune. Dane Fortune. And I believe you do. Whoever killed William and Emily Ransom wanted you dead, too, missy. I saw the death threats."

"First of all, don't call me missy. Second of all, I can take care of myself."

"You may be able to take care of yourself, but—"

She'd had it with this guy. She slammed her glass on the counter and rounded the island. She gave him a push toward the front door. "Thank you for your concern, but I don't need your services."

"Skye, wait."

"Good day, Mr. Fortune."

She shoved him out the door, slammed it and twisted the lock. She didn't have time for this nonsense.

Skye ran back up the stairs and had started packing another box when the doorbell rang again. She huffed out an annoyed breath. Could this guy not take no for an answer?

She bounded down the stairs. When she flung open the door, she stopped short. Conner Dade stood on the porch. He was one of her father's long-time colleagues. What was he doing there?

Actually, it wasn't a mystery. Several of her father's co-workers and colleagues had been by the last few days.

"Conner, hi."

She tried to sound as jovial as possible, figuring that, like so many others the past few days, he wanted to extend his sympathies to her, maybe drop off yet another in a countless procession of consolatory casseroles, most of which now resided in the freezer. Lucy came by with one. Thomas Hardy showed up with a couple bottles of wine. Conner, however, appeared to be empty-handed.

"Skye, I wanted to see how you were doing. I hope I'm not interrupting?" He glanced at her attire and tried hard not to scowl.

Bastard. "I'm packing some of my parent's things. Please come in." Reluctantly, she stepped aside and let him enter. "Can I get you something? Coffee or water?"

She breezed through the entry to the kitchen. Conner stood near the front door, glancing to his left and right. She paused, looked at him over her shoulder.

"Conner?"

"Uh, no thank you."

What the hell was he doing? She watched as he peered into her father's private office just off the main foyer.

"Tea, then?" she asked.

He glanced at her, making eye contact, and forced a smile. He walked to her, took her hands in his and squeezed them.

"As I said, I came to see how you were doing." He hugged her, gripping her so hard she thought she would suffocate. And it was weird. He wasn't the hugging type.

"I'm fine." She pushed out of his embrace. She didn't have time for his phony sympathy.

"Have you decided what to do about the house?" His lips twitched as he said it. He shifted from one foot to the other.

"No, I haven't." She did but it was none of his business.

She wrinkled her brow, wondering what he was up to. Conner Dade had never been close to her father, at least not on a personal level, so what was he doing here now? They were merely colleagues. Her father held Conner in the utmost respect and trusted him, but they weren't exactly chummy. She hadn't seen him since the funeral and before that, almost never. Why this sudden appearance and asking her questions that were none of his business?

"What about your father's research?" Now he cracked his knuckles and paced a small area of the kitchen entryway.

"What about it?" she asked, her eyes narrowed. His demeanor was suspicious.

"I know he kept some notes here about some of the projects he was tinkering with." He stopped pacing, shoved his hands in his pockets.

"Most of those projects are top secret, aren't they?" she asked. "And, anyway, all the notes he had in his office were confiscated by the lab."

"What do you mean?"

"I mean after the funeral, someone from DARPA and the NSA or the CIA or something came with a search warrant..." Her words trailed off as she remembered. She'd put that day out of her mind because she'd still been numb from the double funeral.

Dane had said her father had been receiving death threats. Could her father's research have something to do with that?

There was a team of men, all flashing their government credentials to prove their identity, not that she'd gotten a good look at all of them. They practically ransacked her father's office and took whatever notes they wanted. She hadn't even seen what they were. All she knew was they'd taken several file folders and thanked her for being so cooperative. They must have known she was at a weak moment and would let them have anything they wanted. A cold prickling sensation tickled the back of her neck.

"A search warrant?" Conner asked. "What'd they take?"

She shrugged. "Folders. I'm not really sure."

"Stupid girl," he muttered and turned, as if to leave. But then he spun back around. The smallest gun she had ever seen was clamped in his hand and pointing at her.

The blood drained from her head as her pulse roared in her ears. A sickly feeling crept over her. "Conner, what are you doing?"

"Where is it?" he demanded.

"Where is what?" She held up her hands in surrender. What the hell was he talking about?

"I know it's here. It has to be. I want it."

"I have no idea what you're talking about." She shook her head, looking around for an escape.

"Stay here." He walked backward, heading for the formal living room.

She had no clue what he was up to. A robbery? But why? And what was the *it* he wanted? Anger flared. How dare he come into her house and threaten her? Had she been through enough?

Creeping through the house, she paused at the edge of the living room entrance, watching Conner. He had placed the gun aside and rummaged through the piano bench. Sheet music and books were strewn all over the floor. He lifted the keyboard cover, examined every key, and then looked inside the piano itself.

She wondered if she could reach the gun before he could. Now she suddenly wished she had taken Dane up on his offer of protection. She'd been stupid to turn him away and wished he'd somehow sense she was in trouble and come back.

Conner roared with anger, balling his fist and punching the wall behind him, leaving a nasty indention in the plaster. Her heart rammed in her chest. He was crazy. She couldn't risk confronting him. Running was her only option. She had to get out of the house before he tried to kill her.

Skye took off for the front door but heard Conner's hurried footsteps behind her. He tackled her and they crashed to the marble floor. Her elbow rapped with a loud crunch, and she winced. Conner grabbed her by the hair, yanking her head back and pointing the gun to her temple.

"I want to know where it is," he rasped in her ear. "Tell me now."

She gasped for breath. "I...don't...know..." she began, but he jerked her head.

"Yes, you do!"

"I...I don't know...what you're talking about," she sputtered again.

"Liar!" he shouted in her ear and cocked the gun.

She squeezed her eyes shut, waiting for the inevitable.

"Do you think your parents' deaths were accidents?" Conner asked. "Didn't it occur to you that being killed on the same day, within hours of each other, was a little suspicious?"

It had and she wanted to find out the truth, but everyone had shut her down. Everyone except Dane. He'd confirmed it and yet she had scoffed at him, sent him away.

"Say goodbye, pretty girl," he breathed.

Nothing could save her now. Nothing but the doorbell. As it chimed, she glanced up to see a shadowy figure through the window. She wanted to shout for help but knew it would cost her dearly. The doorbell chimed again.

"Get up." Conner stood, dragging her with him by the arm. He shoved her toward the door. "Answer it and get rid of whoever it is. And quickly."

With a ragged breath, she turned the knob and pulled open the door. Conner stood behind it out of sight, waiting. The postman smiled on the other side of the threshold.

"I have a package I need you to sign for." He handed her a green return-receipt card and a pen.

"Of course." She tried to smile as she took the pen from his hand. Her signature was a scribble. She mouthed the words *help me* as she signed. The postman made no effort to understand her. He took the card from the back of a large envelope, and then handed her the thick letter.

"Have a nice day." He left.

It was her only chance. She had to get out of the house now or Conner was going to kill her. Clutching the letter in one hand, and the edge of the door in her other, she did the only thing she could. She shoved the door backward into Conner as hard as she could, thumping him in the face with the edge. It caught him off guard and he fell back, letting out a startled cry.

Wasting no more time, Skye dashed from the house. Conner was hot on her trail. She glanced over her shoulder, saw him raise the gun and fire.

She cradled the envelope against her body and dropped to the ground, throwing out her hand to break her fall as she hit the pavement. It jarred her from the point of impact to the back of her teeth. The bullet found its way into the side of the postman's truck. The postman, an innocent bystander, spun, his face glazed with shock and his eyes wide. It was the moment of distraction Skye needed to clamber to her feet and make a run for it.

She dashed down the street, refusing to look back.

ARK'S CELL PHONE RANG. He grabbed it from the bedside table and answered the first ring. "Crane."

"Why haven't you killed the girl?" Conner Dade said, his voice gasping and winded.

"What the hell? You told me not to."

"And now I'm telling you I want her dead. Today. Now. And bring me proof of death."

"It'll cost you. Double. All in advance."

"Fine. I'll wire the money tonight. Just kill that girl!" He hung up.

Ark put aside the cell phone and rolled out of bed. The female behind him grumbled at her disturbed sleep. He had met the girl at a bar the night before. He'd put her in an Uber soon enough and send her home.

Shoving aside the bed clothes, he pulled on a pair of boxers and shuffled down the hall to his office. He silently closed the door so he wouldn't be interrupted by his latest conquest. His desk was cluttered with paperwork, but the thick file folder he wanted was right on top. He flipped open the folder and sat in the leather executive chair.

Skye Ransom's picture was where he'd left it last night before hitting the bar. He looked at it often and had the lines of her face memorized. With delicately carved features and perfect, full lips, her unusual indigo eyes bored into him, as though they could see into his soul through the photograph. Her long wavy hair was the color of a shiny new penny.

Ark read over her stats as he lit a cigarette. At five-foot-six, she was athletic, smart and the daughter of one of the wealthiest men in the country. Blowing out a plume of smoke, he ran his finger down the edge of the photo, over the wisps of her hair. It would be a shame to kill her. He'd do it, but it would cost Conner Dade dearly. He would make sure of that.

Skye ran down the street, sweat pouring down her face. Her hand cramped from clutching the envelope. She turned up the first street she came to, and then plunged through an alleyway between houses. She needed time to think and figure out what she was going to do. She dove for cover behind a pair of trash cans and sat on the edge of someone's driveway in the shade of a carport. Dropping the envelope in front of her, she put her head in her hands.

Her chest heaved from exertion. Her legs shook with fatigue and her chest ached from breathing hard. Her hands shook as she dragged her fingers through her tangled coppery hair, yanking out her ponytail. Her sweat-dampened hair stuck to the back of her neck in the oppressive heat.

Whatever Conner was after, he wanted it bad enough to kill her for it. Did he kill her parents, too? His words rang in her ears.

*Do you think your parents' deaths were accidents? Didn't it occur to you that being killed on the same day, within hours of each other, was a little suspicious?*

He had practically confessed, hadn't he? But if he had done it, then how could she prove it? At the moment, all she could prove was he attacked her.

She looked down at the envelope she'd carried away from the house. It had been forwarded from her old apartment address to this one. The handwriting was neat, the penmanship hauntingly familiar. It was her father's. The postmark indicated it had been mailed to her a few days before he died. The packaging was the kind with the bubble wrap already built inside, like someone would use when mailing something fragile.

She shuddered with the cold realization it was a message from the grave.

Curious, Skye tore open the flap. Inside was a sheet of paper folded neatly in half and a small silver object about three inches long. There was a black button and a blank digital readout on one side. She flipped open the note and read her father's message.

*Skye, you don't know what this is and neither does your mother. Hold it for me until I ask you for it. Let no one know you have it. I'll explain what it is very soon.*

He was right about one thing. She had no idea what it was or what it could be. She decided it was time to make a visit to her father's lab. She might not be able to trust Conner Dade, but there was still someone there she could contact.

# Chapter Four
## Out of the Frying Pan...

SKYE ROSE AND BRUSHED off her faded jeans. Thomas Hardy was her only hope in figuring out this mess.

She tossed the envelope in a nearby trash can, then folded the letter and shoved it in her jeans pocket. Clutching the strange, silver object in her hand, she went to the end of the alleyway, pausing at the street, looking both ways. If she was going to make it to the lab, she would need her car. It was too far to make it on foot.

She circled the block, and then went back up the street. Pausing behind a bush, she peered over the leaves. Someone had called the police, and they were milling around the house. Conner and his car were gone. Part of her wanted to go to the police, tell them what had happened with Conner. But she knew she needed hard evidence to connect him to her parents' murders. Evidence she didn't have. Another part of her said she needed to find out more about the object in her hand. Her parents died because of it. She was sure of it. Why else would he mail it to her if he didn't think his life was in danger? Dane said he'd been receiving death threats. This thing in her hand was proof of that.

The question now was how was she going to get to the lab?

Her answer came when a sedan rolled up to the house and Dane Fortune stepped out. He stood on the sidewalk watching the police with his eagle-sharp eyes. She watched him from her vantage point as he took in the scene and wondered why she always looked like shit when he showed up.

Then he looked right at her. Her pulse raced as he gave her a small nod of acknowledgement. He walked back to his car and pulled open the passenger side door, peering at her with a silent invitation to get in the damn car. She made a mad dash for it and dove in. He slammed the door, walked around the front of the car and slid in behind the wheel.

Dane Fortune was calm, cool, collected. Nothing seemed to fluster him.

"What happened?" He nodded toward the police.

"One of my dad's colleagues tried to kill me. For this."

He peered down at the object in her palm. "What is that?"

She shook her head. "I don't know. It was mailed to me in an envelope with my father's handwriting." Gooseflesh erupted on her arms as she said it aloud. It haunted her to think her father sent her the package thinking something horrible might happen to him.

Dane stared at the device for a long, quiet moment. "Is there anyone at this lab you think you can trust?"

He had the same thought she did. She nodded. "Yes."

Dane started the car.

HIDING IN THE CLOSET of the Ransom home's master suite, Conner held his breath and waited for the police to finish searching the place. He didn't intend to leave until he found what he'd come for——the time bender. He was certain it was somewhere close at hand and that William Ransom had hidden it for safekeeping.

Footsteps receded and voices faded, and he knew he was alone in the mansion. It was his time to act. He slipped out of the closet and began to search, dumping out bureau drawers, emptying closets, dismantling beds, and ransacking through boxes and bags. He tore the house apart, upstairs and down, spilling the contents of every desk drawer, cabinet, nook and cranny onto the floor. He ripped paintings off the walls and slashed open the paper backings, searching vainly for hidden contents. Still, he found nothing.

"It has to be here," he muttered nearly an hour later. "Has to be here, has to be here, *it has to be here.*"

His face was hot and flushed, greased with a sheen of nervous sweat. His hair stood askew from where he kept running his fingers furiously through it. Had he looked in a mirror, he probably wouldn't have recognized himself. He would have wondered who the madman was in William Ransom's ravaged living room.

"It has to be here." He kicked a ripped-open sofa cushion sending foam stuffing scattering across the hardwood floor.

But it wasn't there, and he couldn't deny it any longer. He'd already searched William's office and the lab unsuccessfully. Now he'd scavenged through the house in vain. If DARPA or the NSA came calling, they already had the most important research. All of William's notes on the time bender had been here. At least, that's what Conner thought since the notes at the lab recently disappeared.

"Where could it be?" He paced, shoving his splayed fingers through his hair again. "What did you do with it, William, you son of a..."

His voice faded and his eyes widened.

He thought of Skye Ransom and the package she'd received before escaping.

"The package," he whispered. His mouth curled in a dark smile. *Gotcha.*

"THEY'LL NEVER LET US in the lab without clearance," Skye said as Dane drove like a madman through the streets of Arlington.

"How do we get clearance?"

"We don't. It takes months for background checks and clearance to be completed. My father worked on top secret projects—"

"I know. Maybe I can pull some strings. Who's your contact there?"

Who was this guy? How could he possibly pull strings to get top secret government clearance? "Thomas Hardy."

He handed her his cell phone. "Call him. Find out if he's had any strange visitors at the lab."

"Like who?"

"Just call." He ordered it in an authoritative voice that indicated it wasn't up for discussion.

"Goldenrod Research Technology. How may I direct your call?" the receptionist answered.

"Thomas Hardy, please."

"One moment."

The music on hold played in her ear. A few clicks on the line and then Thomas answered. "Hardy."

"Thomas, it's Skye Ransom."

"Skye, where are you? Are you safe?" His voice dropped to a muffled whisper. It sounded like he covered the phone with his hand.

"For the moment," she said.

"Government guys have been here all morning snooping around the lab."

She gave Dane a sideways glance. "What sort of government guys?"

Dane squealed to a stop at the curb. He turned to her as she waited for an answer.

"I don't know. NSA. Maybe CIA and a whole bunch of other folks with three-letter acronyms. They've been asking me and Lucy a lot of questions. They're looking for Conner but he's not here."

Yeah. She knew where Conner was. Dane gave her a hand signal to indicate he wanted her to get on with it.

"Listen, Thomas, I need to come by the lab and show you something."

"What is it?"

"I can't tell you over the phone. I need to show you."

"You don't have clearance—"

"I know, but it's important. Can we meet somewhere?"

Silence as he paused. "I'll try to get out of here. I'll meet you at the old tech building. You remember where that is?"

"Yes."

"Twenty minutes." He hung up.

"Well?" Dane prompted.

"He wants to meet at a place near the corner of North Randolph and 11th Street. You know where that is?"

"Yeah. I know it." He put the car in gear and headed in that direction.

THOMAS WAS WAITING FOR her. He was one of the younger scientists on her father's staff. In his mid-thirties, he had graduated *magna cum laude* with a degree in computer science. Besides Conner Dade and Lucy

Wakefield, he was the only one who had worked closely with her father and would know what he had been researching at the time of his death.

Blond haired and blue eyed, Thomas stood just over six feet tall with a strong square jaw and broad shoulders. They arrived at the place her father referred to as the "old tech building." Thomas said it was where all computers go to die. It was a one-story ramshackle building with blacked out windows. Thomas waited outside the door when they parked.

He eyed Dane as they got out and approached.

"Who's this?" Thomas had a suspicious glint in his eyes.

"Dane Fortune," he replied.

"We can trust him," she said. "Dad did."

It was all Thomas needed. He gave a nod, then punched in the access code to the door. The building smelled like old computer equipment. Old CPUs, flat screen and CRT monitors, laser printers, fax machines, even a dot matrix printer could be found among the ruins of the computer boneyard. Everything was coated in a thick layer of dust from the years of neglect and disuse.

Thomas led them through the shadowy hallways to another door. He used another keypad and then his handprint to open the door to a large back room with black metal miniblinds blocking out every inch of sunlight. An eight-foot table sat in the middle of the room with several computers that looked more new tech than old tech. A large 3D printer dominated one corner, a color copier/printer in another corner. This room had a pungent new-electronic smell that permeated the air, and it was clear to Skye it hadn't been neglected like the rest of the place.

Dane and Skye exchanged a glance.

"Lot of security," Dane commented.

"William wanted it that way. Now what's this about?"

"I need you to tell me what this is." She held the silver object out to him.

Thomas gawked at it as he gently picked it up, holding it in his palm. "Where did you get this?"

"Dad sent it to me. I got it in the mail today. Right before Conner Dade tried to kill me."

His eyes met hers, suddenly looking far too serious, as if what she'd said didn't surprise him in the least.

"It's a good thing you came to me. We have a lot to talk about."

AFTER BEING UNABLE TO find the time bender, a dejected and frustrated Conner went back to his apartment. He closed all the blinds, kept all the lights off and sat in the middle of his bedroom floor. He was convinced Skye had the time bender since there was no other place it could be. He'd searched everything. He had to get it back. She didn't know what she had, and when she tried to use it, it could cause all sorts of mayhem.

He needed it. He had a use for it. She didn't. His plan was to go back to the point in time when he and William Ransom had first struck a deal to work on a time machine together. He'd stolen William's journals from the lab, all of his notes and design schematics for the time bender. Conner would take these with him back in time and leave them for his past self to find and claim.

Then the course of history would change. He would claim the creation and invention of the time bender, not William. Conner would be the one to work with the government entities who were clamoring to get their hands on it. Or he could sell it on the Dark Web for any amount of money he wanted. He'd be the one calling all the shots. Not William.

Either way, he would make millions on the tiny pocket-sized time machine. William was conservative and cautious with his invention, unwilling to let the military get its hands on it, fearful of its use as a possible weapon. But not Conner. He didn't care what it was used for as long as he controlled who used it and when. He could dole out its uses to the highest bidders.

The dollar signs flashed in his eyes. He smiled as he imagined holding the time bender in his hand, running his finger over the digital read-out. In his mind, he twisted the top, turning the machine on. He could almost hear it emit a high-pitched hum and see the read-out glowing the green numbers of today's date. On the bottom was a tiny dial. He imagined twisting it until the numbers read the day William recruited him to help on the top-secret project. Then all he would have to do was push the little black button and all of his dreams would come true.

"Hello, Conner."

Conner's head snapped up, searching through the dimly lit room for the source of the voice. He knew immediately who it was. He recognized the deep baritone. Ark Crane materialized out of the shadows of the bathroom and stood two strides away from him.

Conner glared at him, startled. "What are you doing here?"

"I believe you hired me for another job. I came to make sure you wired the money," Ark replied calmly.

"Did you do it? And if so, where's the proof?" Conner got to his feet.

"That's not how I operate, and you know it," Ark said. "Money first."

"No," Conner said stubbornly. "Death first."

Ark stepped out of the gloom beyond the bathroom doorway. Conner's eyebrows raised as he realized the hitman held a pistol leveled at him.

"You mean to kill me? Before you get your money?" Smug authority stripped from his tone of voice, replaced by anxious fear. "That...that wouldn't be wise."

Ark clamped his hand around Conner's neck, pulling him close. The man coughed, trying vainly to breathe. Ark shoved the muzzle of the gun into his ribs.

"I won't regret killing you, Conner Dade," he whispered roughly. "You play by my rules, you see. Get me the cash, up front, or the deal's off. You have until midnight."

Ark released him then and stepped back, intending to turn and walk away. Conner gasped for breath, rubbing his throat.

"All right," he croaked. "You'll have your money. I'll wire it in half an hour."

"I want proof of the transfer."

"You'll get it," Conner said.

"I better." Ark opened the front door and calmly walked away.

MEANWHILE, AT THE OLD tech building, Skye and Dane pulled up a chair while Thomas sat at the desk. He tapped on one of the computers until the screen came up with a program Skye had never seen before.

"Tell me, Thomas. I need to know everything," she said.

The leather chair creaked with Thomas's weight.

"The day after your father died, I went into his office. It was obvious someone had been there, rummaged through his desk. Will always kept this..." he held up the time bender, "...locked in a metal box. It was open and empty on his desk. I thought it had been stolen."

"Did you report it to the police?" she asked.

"How could I report a secret, privately-funded research project was missing?" He shook his head. "Also, his personal journals with all his research notes were missing. There's really only one person who would take them."

"Conner Dade?" Dane asked.

Thomas nodded. "I thought for sure he'd stolen that, too." He nodded to the small object. "I'm relieved to see he didn't get it. Will and Conner had been feuding for the last few months. Will told me he thought Conner was up to something and that he was going to take this and hide it." He placed the object on the desk in front of him. "He wouldn't tell me what he was going to do. He wanted to keep it secret, away from Conner. He said he was sorry he couldn't tell me. I told him I understood, but I got worried when I found his office had been ransacked."

"What is that thing, Thomas?" Skye eyed the object.

"You really don't know?"

"No. As I said, it came in the mail to me with this." She reached into her pocket and pulled out the crumpled note and passed it to him. He took it, read it over, and then lay it on the desk.

"I think I know what it is," Dane said. "William made me sign a non-disclosure agreement before he'd hire me."

Skye's head snapped in his direction. "You didn't tell me that."

"It wasn't relevant at the time. Now it is." Dane turned back to Thomas, eyeing the small object on the desk in front of him. "It's the time machine, isn't it?"

"Yes." He ran his hand across his stubbled chin. "It's the time machine."

"Excuse me?" Skye's heart stopped at the words. What the devil was her father doing building a time machine? And why the hell did he send it to her?

"Will called it a time bender," Thomas replied.

Her breath caught in her throat. Hearing Thomas say that brought back her father's last words to her the day he was killed. They rang in her ears now.

"That's...oh, my God, Thomas," she whispered. "The day he died...he told me to protect the time bender. He mailed it to me for safekeeping."

"It would seem so." He stood, paced the confines of the office.

"Because he was receiving death threats. The whole family was," Dane added. "He wanted to keep it as far away from Skye and his wife as possible but why mail it to Skye?"

"Yeah. Why mail it to me?"

Thomas shrugged. "I can only guess he thought giving it to you would keep it safe. Maybe he suspected Conner and that was why he had to get it away from the lab."

Dane turned to her. "What was the postmark on that envelope? Do you remember?"

"A few days before he died," she said. "He sent it certified mail, so I'd have to sign for it."

"What was the return address?" he asked.

"I...don't remember." She'd stuffed the envelope in a random trashcan in the alleyway behind someone's house. She'd never thought to look at the return address or the postmarked city. Now she wished she had. "Thomas, how long has he been working on this?"

"A long time. Since your mother was diagnosed with cancer."

"William told me he intended to take his wife forward in time to try to find a cure," Dane said.

Her heart thudded. Her father, bless him, had decided building a time machine would be the answer to her mother's illness, though she couldn't fathom what he intended to do with it. Skye bit her lower lip harder to keep it from quivering. She didn't want to burst into tears here in front of two men she barely knew.

"Yes. Your father planned to try it out on himself, but he never got a chance when things started to go sour between him and Conner."

She looked at Dane, met his crystal blue gaze. "Did Conner hire a hitman to kill my parents?"

"Someone did," Dane said, indicating he wasn't sure who but perhaps had a hunch.

"I believe he's capable of something like that," Thomas said. "He was insanely jealous of everything your father ever did. They had an altercation in the office not too long ago. Conner wanted to try the time bender, but your father was worried it wasn't ready yet for human testing. We had some minor successes moving papers and pens and other things."

"I had no idea about any of this," Skye said.

"No, because it was kept top secret. Only the four of us knew about it." Thomas stood and paced. "Lucy stayed out of the arguments, mostly. She was the one who figured out the whole space-time continuum thing."

Skye stared at him as though he'd grown a second head. "The what?"

"The space-time continuum. The fourth dimension," Thomas explained. "Didn't you ever watch Star Trek?"

She waved away the quip. "I don't care about Star Trek, Thomas. What about this space-time continuum?"

Thomas tapped his chin. "Basically, the time bender bends space and time around whoever is holding it. It creates a doughnut-shaped vacuum bending spacetime on itself. It forms a closed time-like curve to send the person holding the bender back in time. The more laps inside the doughnut, the further back or forward in time you'd go."

"How do you know how many laps you're doing?" Dane asked.

"That's the problem. We haven't been able to figure that out yet. The date dial on the end seems to work but...well, we're not sure if it really does."

"Wouldn't gravitational fields be a factor, too?" Dane asked.

"Yes. They'd have to be strong and precise to form a closed time-like curve," Thomas said with a nod.

Surprise flashed through her as she looked at Dane. "You understood all that?"

"No. Well, a little," he said. "I have a passing interest in physics."

Her response was a lifted eyebrow.

"Plus, we think because the way it bends time, it could open up parallel universes. Really, there's no telling where and when the person using the time bender will end up."

"That's impossible. There's no such thing as parallel universes." This was really sounding more like science fiction than science fact.

Thomas gave her a straight face. "It *is* possible, Skye."

"Maybe in the Star Trek universe," she scoffed, dismissing the idea as ridiculous and trivial.

"At any rate, the bender is still not working right. We had an incident with a mouse." Thomas sounded and looked grim.

"What happened when you used it on the mouse?" she asked.

"We sent the mouse forward in time by a day. It killed it," Thomas said. "Time travel is a tricky thing. There are all kinds of variables to take into consideration——so many unknowns. Every day, the world turns on its axis and rotates around the sun, right?"

She nodded, puzzled, not understanding his point.

"The point on the earth where we're standing right now might not be here in this exact same spot tomorrow," Thomas said. "Or in the next century, or even five minutes from now. There's no guarantee of where you're going to end up. And the earth's geological landscape has changed throughout history. Heck, we're standing someplace that used to be a tropical ocean millions of years ago. You could go back in time and wind up in that ocean, or on another continent. Anywhere." He paused, giving her a pointed look. "Any time."

Skye understood now. An uneasy shiver went through her. "So...where did the mouse wind up?"

"That wall over there." Thomas pointed across the room to a spot she hadn't noticed before. They'd obviously busted out the drywall. It had been recently patched and re-plastered. "*Inside* the wall."

"We went back, made some modifications and adjustments, but your father wasn't ready to test it again yet, much less on a person."

"But Conner was," Dane pointed out.

"Right," he said. "He didn't care about the risks or the problems with the system."

"Problems?" Skye asked.

Thomas nodded grimly. "Our research indicates you can only use the time bender once every seventy-two hours. Once you transport yourself somewhere, you're stuck for a while and then you only have one shot to escape."

"What happens if you miss the window?" Dane asked.

"We don't know the answer to that yet. It's possible the time bender will eventually reset itself."

Skye quietly contemplated this.

"And that's not all," Thomas continued. "The time bender is dangerous. We don't think you can get back to where you started."

"You mean, you can transport yourself to the past—"

"Or future," he interrupted.

"Or future, but you can't get back home?" she asked.

Thomas nodded again. "You'd be trapped forever. Lost somewhere in time."

CONNER'S CELL PHONE RANG as he shoved stacks of bills into a bag. He snatched it up and answered in a clipped tone. "Yeah."

"Where's the money, Dade?" Ark's dark voice rumbled through the phone.

"I ran into a snag."

"Then no deal."

"But I got it. At least part of it," Conner said quickly.

Silence, then the hitman said, "What does that mean?"

"Meet me in Quincy Park at the picnic tables in ten minutes," Conner said.

He hung up before Ark could reply. It was a risk, he knew but one he had to take to make sure Skye was taken out of the equation. Zipping the bag, Conner slung it over his shoulder and headed down the street. The meeting place was a quick walk from his apartment building.

Conner's heart was in his throat. What he was about to do would most likely get him killed once Ark figured it out. He hoped the man would be trusting and not count the money until after Skye was dead.

Conner made his way to the picnic tables, glancing left and right. The park was busy with joggers, dog-walkers, mothers and their kids on the playground. Even a few tennis players. Not a very private place for a murder, if that's what Ark was thinking. The man was nowhere in sight.

Conner's cell phone vibrated, startling him. He reached for it, quickly answering. "I'm here."

"Turn around," Ark said.

Conner did and spotted him across the park, phone to his ear. He wore dark sunglasses to hide his eyes and a ballcap to shadow his face. Clever.

It would keep the park security cameras from easily spotting him should he attempt to kill him.

"What's in the bag?" Ark asked.

"A deposit. It's all I could get my hands on. The rest will be transferred to your offshore account once the girl is handled."

"What are you trying to pull, Dade? I don't want cash. I want the money wired, as we discussed."

"I'll double the amount once it's done."

A pause, then, "Drop the bag by the trashcan and back away."

Conner did as he was ordered.

"I'll be in touch." *Click.*

ARK ARRIVED BACK AT his apartment. He tossed the bag on the floor, then crouched and unzipped it. He grabbed the first stack of bills on top and quickly thumbed through them.

The first few on top were legitimate twenty-dollar bills. Underneath those were blank pieces of heavy bond paper cut to match the same shape and size as currency. Conner had duped him.

Now he would have to get even.

CONNER DADE WOKE UP when Ark pressed the gun to his temple.

"You're dead." Ark nudged his head with the muzzle of the gun.

Conner scrambled to his feet, hands out. "Crane, I can explain—"

"Shut up," Ark interrupted. "Did you think I wouldn't check it?"

Sweat beaded Conner's forehead as the hitman cocked his gun.

"Wait. You need me," Conner said.

"Why?"

"Because I can lead you to the girl. She has something I want. She'll have questions about it. I know where she'll go to get answers. I can take you to her. Easiest job you'll ever have."

"Where?"

"The lab."

Ark removed the gun. "Then let's go."

# Chapter Five
## ...and Into the Fire!

SKYE STARED AT THE offensive little device as though it was radioactive material. The look on her haggard face said it all. She sagged against the chair, still in her filthy clothes. Her jeans had holes in the knees. Her sneakers had seen better days. Dane couldn't help but have a pang of sympathy for the girl. She'd been through so much losing her parents and now there was some madman after her.

He wasn't so sure he was all for this time machine thing either, but he had to admit the idea was genius. William Ransom's heart was in the right place when he created it, but it could be a terrible weapon in the wrong hands. Hands like Conner Dade. Anyone who wanted to wipe out an entire family had an evil agenda all his own.

Skye was collateral damage in this war between the now-dead William Ransom and Conner Dade. The only thing Dane couldn't figure out was why kill them all.

"What am I supposed to do with it?" Skye asked, peering at the time bender.

"Your father sent it to you for a reason," Thomas said.

"Yeah, to protect it, but I don't want it. I don't want anything to do with it." She shook her head.

A text came through on Thomas's phone. His head snapped up after he read it. "Lucy says Conner was looking for me."

A beep sounded on his computer, and they all stared at the computer. "Someone's here." Thomas got to his feet.

Skye sucked in a sharp breath. "It's Conner."

Dane unholstered his gun. "Is there a backway out of here?"

"There is, but you won't be needing it." Conner Dade appeared in the doorway, a hulking giant of a man behind him.

Skye jumped to her feet. Dane shoved her behind him. Thomas moved to stand next to him, creating a human barrier between her and Conner.

"All I want is the time bender." Conner's gaze pierced through him to Skye. "She has it. I know she does."

"She doesn't," Dane answered.

Conner's jaw was set in a grim line as he looked at him. "Who the hell are you?"

Dane pointed his gun at the man. "Doesn't matter, does it?"

The hulking man behind Conner moved to stand next to him, a gun in his hand. "Drop the gun."

Before anyone could say anything, a shower of bullets shattered the wall of windows behind them. They all ducked behind the desk, huddling on the floor. Dane tackled Skye, keeping her safe from the flying shards and bullets. Even Conner and Ark dropped to the ground.

"What is *happening*?" Her voice was a rough whisper.

"There must be an interested third-party," Dane said. "We'll need that backway out of here now."

Thomas reached the time bender still on his desk and slid it across the floor to Skye. She grabbed it, clutching it in her fist. "Get out of here."

"What about you?" Skye asked.

More bullets. One took out his monitor, which made it pop and explode in a shower of sparks. Dane popped his head up to see where Conner and the hitman were, but they were nowhere in sight.

"They're gone. We can all go," he said.

"I can't leave the equipment. There's too much sensitive data—"

Another round of attacks. A bullet grazed Thomas's shoulder as Dane pushed Skye closer to the floor.

"Go. Through that door." Thomas nodded to a door behind them. "The code is 2319."

"Thomas—" she started.

"Just go. It'll take you to the back of the building and out." He jumped to his feet and yanked an external hard drive out from the USB port. "Come on."

Dane took her by the arm and helped her to her feet. Together, they fled the old tech building. Skye punched the code into the keypad of the door and then shoved it open. They ran down a long, dark hallway but could see a brightly light red sign indicating EXIT.

She barreled into the door, pushing it open and they exited into the bright afternoon sunshine in the back of the building, just like Thomas said. She halted, put her hands on her knees. Her breath see-sawed in and out.

"Now what?" she panted. "And why aren't you winded?"

"I keep in shape."

He peered up and down the alleyway looking for a quick escape route. Without a car, there wasn't one. At the end of the alley, a black car turned down it and headed straight for them. He gave her a shove.

"We gotta move."

She saw the sedan as he shoved her and broke into a run. He followed her, but the car was gaining at a rapid pace. Ahead of them, the hitman came out a second back door, turned and aimed. She squealed. Dane shoved her toward the building, shielding her as he fired round after round at the hitman.

Behind them, the car closed the gap and suddenly came to a tire-squealing halt. The driver's door popped open, and a woman stuck her head out.

"Get in!"

"Lucy, thank God!"

"You know her?" Dane asked.

"Yes, come on."

Skye bounded toward the car and jumped in the back. Dane took the passenger side. He rolled down the window and stuck out his gun, aiming at the henchman but he seemed to have given up.

For now.

"How did you know?" Skye asked.

Lucy put it in reverse and floored it, backing out of the alleyway with the speed and skill of a race car driver.

"Conner was sniffing around looking for Thomas. I know he and Will had a falling out. I also know he broke into Will's office and stole his journals."

"That's what Thomas said, too."

"The NSA and some guys from DARPA have been at the lab all morning, too." The woman barreled out of the alleyway, spun the car and headed down the street. "They're looking for the time bender."

"You know that for certain?" Dane asked.

"Yes." She looked at him. Smiled. "Because I sold them the information."

The woman was shady, too?

"Where is it, Skye?" Lucy looked at her in the rearview mirror.

"I don't know what you're talking about."

She played dumb. Good girl.

"It wasn't in William's office or the lab. So where is it?"

On impulse, Dane reached for the wheel, jerked it hard toward the right making it spin out of control. From the backseat, Skye yelped. Lucy struggled to regain control of the car from Dane. He didn't want to shoot her, so he elbowed her in the side of the head, knocking her out.

But the car continued to careen down Washington Boulevard past Quincy Park. He aimed for the sidewalk, hoping to slow it down.

"Hang on," he told Skye.

The car popped the curb, bounced and then smashed into the corner of a cleaners, destroying the front end and demolishing the storefront. Startled customers and the girl behind the counter scattered, terrified looks on their faces. At least the car was stopped. He ignored the people in the cleaners and looked over the back of the seat at her.

"You all right?"

She nodded, picking herself up off the floorboard. "Dane, I don't understand. I thought my father trusted these people."

"He did. But they're dirty."

Except for maybe Thomas, the computer guy.

Dane pushed open the door. "We can't stay here."

She got out, stood next to him on the sidewalk.

They both saw the hitman coming for them at the same time. She huffed out an annoyed breath. "Is this guy superhuman or what? How did he find us?"

"Don't know." He grabbed her hand, and they took off.

DANE DRAGGED SKYE DOWN the crowded sidewalk as they dodged pedestrians. As a jogger, she should be used to all this running, but she wasn't. She was winded, the race of adrenaline throbbing through her veins and fear twisting her stomach into a tight knot.

A bullet flew past her head. Dane shoved her toward a building for cover. He shielded her, turned and fired back.

"What are we going to do?" she asked, out of breath.

He glanced up at the store they'd stopped in front of. It was, oddly, a costume shop.

"In here."

He gave her a push inside. A cheerful chime jingled, announcing their arrival. But there was nothing cheerful about their arrival in the least. Skye sagged against the door while Dane kept a watchful gaze on the street.

"Hide," he ordered.

She blinked, uncertain she heard him correctly. "What?"

He waved her into the store. "Find someplace to hide. He wants you, not me."

"But—"

"William hired me to protect you, Skye, so let me do my job."

She gulped in a deep breath and nodded.

The shop was not a modern one. It was a specialty clothing store with handmade medieval costumes divided by century on one side. On the other, costumes from popular movies and TV shows as well as the standard vampire, witch, ghost. A short bald man came from a back room and greeted her with a broad smile while Dane continued to stand at the window, gun in hand. She blocked the salesclerk's view of Dane so he wouldn't see the gun.

"Good afternoon. How can I help you?" He spoke in a thick British accent.

She pasted on her best smile. "Hi, there! Do you have anything medieval-ish?" A silly question, she knew, but she was trying to keep the clerk busy and not focused on Dane.

"Are you looking for something in particular?" he asked.

"Oh, you know, just something I can wear to an upcoming costume party for work."

"Right this way."

He led her through the shop to a rack devoted to gowns that looked like something from a Renaissance festival. He pulled a midnight blue dress in velvet off the rack and held it up.

"This would go beautifully with your coloring."

"Great! Can I try it on?"

He motioned to the dressing room off to the left. She ducked inside, closing the flimsy wood door and sliding the lock. She clutched the dress to her chest, straining her ears to listen for any sound coming from the front of the store. She heard the clerk talking to Dane and then Dane responding in a terse tone of voice. She couldn't make out the words, but it didn't sound friendly.

The door chime sounded. Then a scuffle. Skye pulled the dress on over her clothes and huddled against the corner of the dressing room, still clutching the time bender. She'd never opened her fist since Thomas slid it to her.

Was Thomas a bad guy, too? Or could she trust him? She didn't know.

She heard a voice outside the dressing room door, an unmistakable baritone that made her blood run cold. The baritone voice belonged to the hitman. A *pop, pop* of gunfire, a thunk as if a body hit the floor. She gasped, covering her mouth with her hand.

"Where's the girl?" the hitman said.

Her hand gripped tighter around the little machine and suddenly it buzzed in her hand. She flexed her fingers enough to see the tiny screen had come alive with numbers in green. But part of them were faded out and she couldn't tell what the numbers were. A date?

The door to the dressing room crashed inward making it splinter into a thousand pieces. Skye flattened her body as much as she could against the mirror. The hitman filled up every inch of the door, glaring down at her with dark, terrible eyes. He reached for her, nearly had his hand on her, when he flew back, and Dane was suddenly there.

Dane threw a punch, knocking the guy back a step or two. But he was bigger and meaner. He came back with a punch of his own that landed on Dane's jaw. Dane stumbled backward into the dressing room bumping into Skye.

Her hand closed in reflex around the time bender. There was a sudden crackle of light and a strange hissing sound, and she realized she'd accidentally pushed the black button. Thomas Hardy's words echoed immediately in her mind...

*Trapped forever...lost somewhere in time...*

...and she felt her heart come to a shuddering, horrified halt.

And then there was nothing at all.

# Chapter Six
## Step Back in Time

SKYE WASN'T SURE HOW long she was out. It seemed like days, judging by the way her head ached. Moaning, she rolled her head from side to side, trying to make sense of the noises and odors around her.

It smelled damp, like wet leaves and the ground felt hard and cold. Her hands rustled beneath her. Yep, wet leaves. She opened her eyes, blinked several times.

Gnarled tree limbs formed a canopy above her. Inky blackness pressed her. A shiver of fear went through her. She sat up and her head objected to the sudden movement.

She groaned. Where was she? What happened?

She tried to stumble to her feet, her aching body protesting, but tripped over the gown. She managed to catch herself, her hand landing on crumbling tree bark of a fallen log and something slimy. She squealed, snatching her hand away, staggering backwards and falling. She crashed into more damp leaves, her rump firmly striking the ground, jarring her and making her teeth rattle.

There was a flutter of wings overhead. Apparently, she had startled birds roosting from their slumber. As she collected herself to try to stand again, she felt something cold and sharp against her cheek.

"Dinna move," said a thick brogue behind her.

Her heart stopped in her chest, her breath caught in her throat. She was afraid to breathe at all. Her skin felt hot, prickly, like she would pass out at any moment. Sure thing. There was no way in hell she was going to move. Not with whatever that was jabbing her in the jowls.

"Please," she whispered, hoping whoever the man was, he had somewhat of a heart. Though *please what* she had no idea.

The jabbing thing moved quickly away and then there was a shuffling of leaves near her feet. Big, strong hands grabbed her by the arms and lifted her as if she weighed nothing. The man flung her over his shoulder and carried her out of the copse of trees.

He had muscles of the likes she had never seen. A body builder? But that didn't explain the thick brogue when he spoke. Maybe she was having a weird dream.

He dumped her to the ground and stood back, his fists on his hips as he glared at her. His long brown hair was plaited into two braids, one on either side of his face, and cascaded over his shoulders. He wore a tartan over one shoulder of his sleeveless tunic, pants and well-worn boots that had definitely seen better days.

"Just what do ye think yer doin'?"

"Excuse me?" She blinked at him in surprise. What was that supposed to mean?

"Ye canna be out alone," he continued. "The roads are no' safe."

"Yeah, well, I think I can take care of myself." She rose, brushing off her skirt. She wasn't about to let some big bawdy man tell her what to do. "Thanks for the concern, but I've got to get going." She took two steps, but he snatched her by the arm. His hand bit into her fleshy upper arm.

"Ye'll be doin' no such thing," he stated matter-of-factly.

"Hey, let me go." She glared at him and tried to jerk free, but he held fast.

"I'm taking ye back to the castle, Alanna," he said.

"I think you have the wrong girl, pal." She poked him in the chest with her index finger. "Now let me go."

"I dinna think ye should be talking to me that way." He grabbed her now by both arms and tugged her toward him. "Do ye have any idea what could happen to ye out here? The English are everywhere."

"The English?" she repeated. What was he talking about?

"Aye." He released her then, looking her up and down with bright blue eyes, making her uncomfortable. It was like he scrutinized her. "I dinna know what yer doing out here, Alanna, but we best be gettin' back to the castle."

"I don't think so." She shook her head. "And by the way, don't touch me again. Now, if you'll excuse me..."

She turned on her heel, started to go. But go where, she hadn't a clue. She had taken two more steps when he charged and snatched her. He flung her over his shoulder once again.

"Ye give me no choice, lassie. I have to take ye back in this undignified manner."

"Hey! Put me down!"

"Ye continue wailin' and ye'll be getting a thrashing when we return," he warned.

A thrashing? Was he kidding? Who the hell was this guy?

Her mind raced, trying to make sense of this weirdness. The last thing she remembered... Wait. What *was* the last thing she remembered?

She and Dane had been running for their lives from the hired killer. The man Conner hired to kill her parents. They entered a costume shop after crashing the car. Dane told her to hide because the hitman followed.

She had a gown under the guise of trying it on while she hid in the dressing room as Dane confronted the guy. But something happened then. What was it?

Oh, crap.

She remembered then. She'd been holding the time bender clutched in her hand because she couldn't get to her pockets. Dane and the hitman crashed through the dressing room door. The hitman tried to grab her. Dane intervened. Then there was a bright flash of light, and she'd lost consciousness.

She pushed the button by accident.

And now the time bender—

Her eyes flew to the copse of trees quickly disappearing in the distance. Oh, crap!

She must have dropped it when she landed, and it had been too dark for her to notice. And now this stranger with the thick brogue was taking her away from it, calling her Alanna. He thought she was someone else.

She craned her neck to glance over him. The castle he spoke of was ahead. She was partially relieved to know the forest of trees was nearby. Perhaps by morning, she could get away and look for the time bender. But what happened to Dane and the hitman?

The man carried her through the castle gate. It quickly closed behind them. He deposited Skye on the ground, her feet squishing in mud. She was cold. Her breath exhaled in white plumes and her teeth chattered. It amazed her that these men didn't seem even slightly affected.

"I see ye found the wee lassie, Malcolm," a loud voice boomed.

The burly Scotsman looked over as three men walked toward them. They all wore tartans and tunics, like the man, Malcolm. The older one in the center, who had called out, now smiled broadly at Skye. Two younger men flanked him, and they exchanged glances she couldn't read. Skye gripped her elbows, trying to keep from shivering.

"Aye, I found her." Malcolm gave her a dark glance, as if she were a child who had disobeyed her parents.

"Is she all right then?" the older man asked.

"She seems well enough," Malcolm replied, not averting his gaze.

"What's wrong with you?" Skye suddenly snapped. "Stop staring at me."

The three men stopped, the older one now gaping wide-eyed at her. "The lassie's got a fire in her, eh?" He chuckled then. "I'll send a message to the Bruce she's unharmed."

The Bruce? Skye's mind raced. What was going on?

"Take the lassie inside, Malcolm, before she freezes to death."

"Stop calling me that," Skye said. "I am no lassie." With her fist balled, she fixed an angry stare at the older man.

"Ye shouldna be talking to a clan leader that way," Malcolm warned. "Especially Campbell."

"I don't care who he is," she spat. "I have to get out of here. I have to get home."

"Calm down, now." Campbell put his arm around her, hugging her. It made her feel like a small child. "Ye are home now, lassie. The Bruce will be wanting to know yer all right. Now let's get ye inside by the fire before ye freeze to death. Come, Malcolm."

Reluctantly, she allowed him to take her inside. With Malcolm on his heels, Campbell shuffled her up a stone staircase, down a drafty hallway and to a small room with a comfortable bed and a blazing fire.

"Get some rest, lassie," he said. "Ye've had a busy day."

The door clicked closed behind her, leaving her alone.

Outside, Ewan Campbell stationed two men at the door to make sure the woman was guarded at all times. He motioned for Malcolm to come with him downstairs to the great hall. Malcolm stood by the hearth staring down into the fire while Campbell helped himself to more ale.

"I dinna think she's Alanna." Malcolm's eyes were still riveted on the fire because he could not look Campbell in the face and tell him his suspicions. "Though her resemblance is uncanny, she doesna act like she should."

"Aye." Campbell sipped his ale. "We'll wait 'til the others come back. Ye think the lassie to be an imposter then?"

"Aye, I do."

"What's become of the real Alanna Douglas, then?" Campbell mused.

"I dinna ken."

Malcolm could attest to the fact she was an imposter by the odd way she acted. No woman would speak to him—or any man—in such a manner. He found her feisty attitude intriguing and endearing and quite unlike the Alanna he knew. The resemblance to the real Alanna, though, was astounding.

When they had received word Robert Bruce's future bride had been kidnapped, he had asked Malcolm if he and his men would search for her. She had been on her way to meet Robert and prepare for their upcoming wedding. He had been introduced to Alanna Douglas once before, knew her kinsman quite well in fact. So, it had come as a surprise when he found a woman who looked much like her in the woods. A woman he'd quickly come to realize was not Alanna at all. Who she was and how she got there, he had no idea. He turned now, his hands behind his back.

"We havna time for this nonsense, Campbell."

"Robert asked us to find her and watch over her, so we will." He took a healthy swig of ale, spilling the liquid down his chin.

"And what are we to do with her at Stirling Bridge?" Malcolm demanded. "She canna come on the battlefield."

"Nor will she," Campbell greed. "They will have wed by then."

Before Malcolm could reply, the doors burst open, and a young man bolted inside. He stumbled before falling to his knees at Ewan's feet, trying to catch his labored breath.

"Campbell," he panted. "I found her."

Campbell and Malcolm exchanged a surprised glance.

"Found who?" Campbell asked.

"Alanna Douglas," the boy gasped. "She's...she's...dead!"

"Dead?" Campbell thumped his mug on the table. "Are ye sure, Hamish?"

"Aye." The boy got to his feet. "We brought her body back with us." He thumbed toward the door.

"Let's have a look then." Campbell rose, followed the boy out the door with Malcolm on his heels.

The girl's body was covered with a white shroud. Campbell pulled back the material and they all stared down at her pretty face. She had been abused before she died. Her skin bore the marks. Her left cheek was covered in bloodied scratches and her neck had bruises. Her hair was a tangled mess with leaves and grass sticking out everywhere.

"*Och*. The poor wee lassie," Campbell said. "'Tis the work of the English. Only they could be so cruel."

"Ye think they killed her?"

"To stop the wedding, aye. I wouldna put it past them." Campbell covered her face again, then addressed the men. "Take her down to the crypt."

Malcom and Campbell watched as they took the girl's body away.

"What now?" Malcolm asked. "Do we tell Robert?"

"We willna tell him just yet." Campbell tapped his finger against his chin.

Malcolm narrowed his gaze. "What are ye thinking?"

"There must be a way to make sure this wedding continues. The other girl bears a striking resemblance to Alanna. Or did ye no' notice?"

"*Och*, I noticed. I ken what yer thinking. Ye think that's wise?" Malcolm asked.

"I do. We should speak to her soon." Campbell clapped Malcolm on the shoulder. "Or perhaps ye should be doin' the talking."

"Why me?" Malcolm scowled.

"Why?" Campbell chuckled. "Because, Malcolm Wallace, tell me ye canna see the girl is smitten with ye?"

If SKYE HAD HEARD Ewan Campbell tell Malcolm she was smitten with him, she would have laughed out loud. At the moment, she was more preoccupied with the fact she seemed to have transported herself back in time and was now without the time bender.

With her hands clasped behind her back, she paced a line on the floor. At least she still had her regular clothes and sneakers on under the dress. That would give her some mobility in this strange unfamiliar world. The only good thing out of this whole mess was that she seemed to be dressed properly, and the men believed she was someone else.

Perhaps that was something she could use to her advantage. She was desperate to get out of there and find the time bender and Dane before someone else did. Where was Dane? What had happened to him? Had he been transported back in time, too? If so, she had to find him, too, though she had no idea how. He was now the only person in the world she could trust. He'd been her only ally, and she hardly knew the man.

And what of the hitman? What happened to him?

She stopped pacing, suddenly recalling Thomas Hardy's admonition against using the time bender.

*We don't think you can get back to where you started. You'd be trapped forever, lost somewhere in time.*

Would she be stuck here in the past? It was essential she found the time bender. And she had less than seventy-two hours to do it, if Thomas was right. As she contemplated her dilemma, the door to her chamber opened. Malcolm stood in the entrance with that scowl still on his face. He hadn't been gone long at all and she was somewhat miffed by his audacity.

"Shouldn't you knock on a lady's door?"

Without answering, he slammed the door shut and took two giant steps to her. His strong hands clamped on her arms and jerked her toward him.

"Now, lassie, 'tis time for ye to be telling me who ye really are."

# Chapter Seven
## Malcolm

DANE GROANED. SOMETHING SHARP and pointy jabbed him in the back and he rolled to his side, reaching behind him. It was a large misshapen rock. Growling, he swiped it off the ground and tossed it away. His head pounded, throbbing with pain.

He sat up and surveyed his surroundings. He was in the middle of a large field, alone. He put his hand to his aching head. When he pulled it away, blood smudged his fingers. Stumbling upright, he staggered down the knoll, but his feet went faster than he could control. One knee buckled under him, causing him to fall, rolling down the hill. When at last he stopped, his cheek pressing into the cool grass, he lay still with this left ankle throbbing like mad. He'd twisted it in his fall and knew he'd likely sprained it. Using the heels of his hands, he pushed to a sitting position. This time, his body was less forgiving from the movement. He had never hurt so badly in his entire life.

Where was he? This sure wasn't the shop they'd entered in downtown Arlington. The last thing he remembered had been punched by the hitman. He'd fallen into the dressing room, colliding with Skye. There had been a blinding flash of light, then...

Then what? He had no idea.

He got to his feet again and reeled before he staggered forward. His left ankle refused to allow him to walk, as if it had a mind of its own. He stumbled again and, rather than fall, he lowered his beat-up body to the ground.

The sudden thunder of horses startled him. Glancing up, he saw the riders crest the ridge, their horses pounding down the sloping knoll heading straight for him. Their appearance was so swift it gave him little time to make a dash for it. Not that he could anyway. He couldn't run with his injured ankle. All he could do was hope he wouldn't be trampled.

"Hold!"

Dane had only seen armor in the movies. He had to admit, theirs was impressive. What was this? A Renaissance festival or something? How did he end up here instead of the shop? The leader stepped down off his horse and towered over him, glaring with beady blue eyes.

"Scottish scum," he spat, his accent lilting and British. "Get off the ground."

"Sorry, can't," Dane said, bewildered. "I'm not part of your show. I think I sprained my ankle. You got a cell phone on you?"

Still glowering, the English soldier kicked him in his injured leg. Dane cried out, crumpling to his side. "You...son of a bitch!"

"Pick him up," the armored soldier ordered. "Drag him if necessary. We'll take him to the next town. We've no time to waste. There is a wedding as we speak, and I must claim my noble right from the bride."

Two men dismounted. One tied Dane's wrists together.

"You can't do this to me," Dane said through clenched teeth. Pain splintered through him as the rope cut into his skin.

"If you cooperate," the leader said, "I will see to it you have medical attention when we arrive. If not, then we will kill you now."

Horrified, Dane watched as his bound wrists were tied to a rope and held by one of the men like a leash. He'd have to run alongside the horse with his bad ankle. Not ideal. He had a good idea what had happened to him. Skye had used the time bender and transported them both back in time. But, where was she?

As he tried to figure it all out, he heard a loud roar of voices. A pack of kilted men, swords raised, suddenly appeared, running toward them.

"Ambush!" the leader shouted.

The mounted English soldiers quickly alighted, faced them head on with swords drawn. Dane struggled with his knots, trying to loosen his hands enough to untie his wrists. The clash of swords rang out around him followed by the smell of blood, the sound of screams of agony.

The horses, spooked from the noise, galloped away. Dane narrowly missed being trampled. He stumbled away, falling again as dirt clods flew around him. He was exposed to the fighting.

At last, he managed to work his hands free. His wrists were raw and rope-burned. He had to get away from there as quickly as possible.

"MacDougal, he's getting away!"

He heard the shout rise above the din in a thick brogue and glanced over his shoulder to see several tartan warriors breaking away and running toward him. The ground was littered with dead English soldiers. The Scotsmen had won the skirmish.

Dane struggled to his feet, wincing as the pain in his ankle flared, sending a white-hot sting through him. He broke into a limping run up the small hill but could hear the men behind him closing the distance.

Looking back again, he saw the tower of a man near him. He braced himself as the man tackled him, knocking him to the ground once more. He smelled of sweat and ale. Dane elbowed him in the abdomen. The man grunted, rolling to his side.

Dane crawled desperately toward freedom. He spied a copse of trees and headed there to hide until it was safe. A sword jabbed abruptly in the ground in front of him, making him pause. He looked up into the fierce blue eyes of another warrior.

"Dinna think ye be leavin' so soon," he said. "MacDougal, come tie up the English."

"No. You can't tie me up again," Dane said. "I'm injured." He swallowed the lump in his throat, annoyed he had resorted to begging. That was not Dane Fortune. But he was definitely out of his element and knew it. Survival was all that mattered now. Survive and find Skye.

The tall Scotsman eyed him with a thoughtful eye. Perhaps contemplating what to do with him.

"I was a prisoner of the...English," Dane continued. He could play their little game, whatever it was...at least until he figured out how to find Skye and the time bender and get out of there.

"Aye," the man said slowly. "Ye dinna sound like the English. What do ye think, MacDougal?"

He hoped they'd let him go, though he wasn't sure he could convince them he was no threat.

"We'll take him to Malcolm," MacDougal said. "He will know what to do with the stranger."

Dane stifled an inward groan. So much for freedom.

"Aye. That's what we'll do then."

MALCOLM'S EYES BORED INTO Skye. His hands were hot as coals on her arms. Her inner voice told her she should be afraid, but she managed to shove it down and out of her mind. With her jaw clamped shut, she pushed him away and stepped back, hands on slender hips. She glared right back, unfazed by his fierce look.

"You know who I am." She said it calmer than she felt and flicked her hair over her shoulder. "I'm Alanna."

"Alanna," he repeated. His eyes narrowed to slits. "Tell me who your da is then."

Her da? Her mind raced to try to interpret what he meant. He didn't give her a chance to figure out an answer before he was spitting another question at her.

"And why do ye speak strangely?"

"*I* speak strangely?" she repeated. "What about you?"

She examined his handsome but battle-scarred face. His hair was dark and thick, his eyes hard. His upper body was muscular, and not from lifting weights. No. Strength like that came from manual labor. Maybe even from killing by the looks of him. He was someone not to be trifled with, to fear. Yet she was willing to believe a woman could soften his brusque exterior. So, she did what any female would do. She pulled out all her feminine tools and stepped toward him, smiling sweetly.

"Let's not argue about anything, Malcolm." She fluttered her dark lashes. "I'd rather get to know you."

His jaw flexed, either from sudden arousal or irritation. She wasn't sure which. She placed her hands on his chest, felt his strength and nearly swooned for real. It had been too long since she felt the power of a man beneath her hands.

"Kiss me, Malcolm. You know you want to."

She tipped her head toward his, her lips slightly parted, expecting his kiss. His face was rough with stubble, lined from long days in the sun. A moment of indecision flashed through his eyes before he shoved her away.

"No. I willna be kissing ye." He stepped back away from her. "Tell me who ye are, for the real Alanna is dead."

"Dead?" There went her idea of impersonating the girl.

"Aye," he replied. "One of our clansmen found her body not more than an hour ago and delivered her hence to show us in proof."

Well, that was rotten luck. So much for that idea. "What happened to her?"

"She was murdered by the English, no doubt." Malcolm folded his arms across his chest. "Ye dinna know who did it, do ye?"

"*Me?*" The word came out a squeak. Was he accusing her of something? She shook her head, her coppery hair bouncing on her shoulders. "How should I know? I don't even know who she was." She paused thoughtfully, then said, "Who was she anyway?"

"She was promised to the King of Scotland," he said. "Or he will be king rather."

She felt the blood drain from her face. "What's his name?"

"Robert Bruce. When he learns his bride is dead, there will be hell to pay."

Skye gasped, holding her hand to her mouth. Robert Bruce...or better known as Robert the Bruce. That was the man to which Campbell referred. Her mind whirled with what little historical fact she recalled. When did Robert the Bruce rule? Wasn't it the thirteenth century? Twelve-something-or-other, right?

"What's your name?"

"Malcom Wallace."

"And...what year is it?"

He looked at her as though she had grown another head.

"Have ye lost yer senses, lassie?"

"Just answer me, please!" she snapped.

"The year of our lord, 1297," he said slowly.

In a sudden whoosh, the blood drained from her head. She faltered back a step. She saw dark pinpricks in her vision and her stomach cramped. It couldn't be, could it? She had *actually* transported herself back in time. She'd used the time bender for real. Now that the truth was confirmed, she was even more worried. What was she going to do? How would she get back home?

"Are ye all right, lass?" he asked and was at her side in a moment. "Ye look a bit pale."

"I'm...great. Just great."

"Are ye English?" he asked.

"Yes. I mean, no. I mean...I don't know."

She sat down hard on the bed, trying to recall her World History. Coach Bowden had been her teacher in high school and he'd droned on and on about things. He never really touched on the war with Scotland and England. Of course, he never really touched on anything. Come to think of it, she couldn't recall the class at all.

Coming back to her senses, she looked at Malcolm again. He had a handsome yet roughened face. What would it do to the historical timeline with her being there? How would it alter the future?

She struggled to remember everything Thomas told her but was drawing a blank. She was more concerned with getting the time bender and getting home. *If* she could get home.

She groaned as she lay on the bed and drew up her knees. Malcolm still looked at her with knit brows. After a long, scowling moment, he headed for the door.

"Perhaps ye need a rest, lassie," he said. "When I return, I expect some answers."

He banged the door closed behind him. But Skye didn't really notice. She curled into the fetal position and fell asleep, hoping that when she awoke, she would be in her own bed, and this would all be a bad dream.

# Chapter Eight
## Bargaining Chip

CAMPBELL CAUGHT MALCOLM IN the great hall after he'd left the girl in her chamber. "Well? What did the lassie have to say?"

"I dinna ken," Malcolm replied.

"What do ye mean by that?" Campbell pressed.

"She doesna ken who Alanna was," Malcolm explained. "But her manner of speech is strange. I canna say where she comes from."

"Is she English then?" Campbell questioned. "Did she kill Alanna?"

"I dinna think so," Malcolm replied. "Robert will be here soon with my brother and then we can tell him what happened."

"Mayhap we should tell him about the look-alike girl."

"I dinna think he will want to marry an imposter."

"The future of Scotland rides on her, Malcolm. We must convince him to go through with the ruse."

"What about the girl?"

"We must convince her, too."

Malcolm could only think this plan was folly. He knew Robert was to marry a woman of noble birth so he could claim the throne from England's King Edward and rule Scotland. Malcolm understood all too well how important it was to see it through. With the real Alanna dead, would the look-alike girl go through with the marriage?

When Alanna had been found murdered, it occurred to Malcolm that the entire arrangement was a trick and Edward Longshanks had no intention of turning over Scotland so easily. Their plans to attack Stirling Bridge would have to be accelerated.

"'Tis why we must be careful." Malcolm paced the length of the great hall with long slow steps.

A messenger came into the great hall and announced riders approached.

"That'll be my brother and Robert," Malcolm said.

"I'll go greet them and bring them here," Campbell said.

Malcom gave a nod as the laird headed away.

SKYE AWOKE, DISCOVERING TO her annoyance she was not dreaming, and she was, indeed, still in the past. She was living the nightmare. She shivered in the gown she had accidentally borrowed from the little shop keeper back home. At least she still had her regular street clothes underneath. That gave her some comfort.

Would she ever see home again?

She had no idea if she would make it out of this world alive. Sliding off the edge of the bed, she stood, knowing she had to retrieve the time bender and get out of there. She wished she had a way to contact Thomas to find out if it would work. She hoped it did. She really didn't want to be stuck there forever.

She cracked the door open and peered out into the drafty hallway. Two men still flanked the door, and both gave her the side eye.

"Oh, hi. I was...looking for Malcom. He said to meet him in the kitchen when I was ready to eat."

They stared at her, mute, for a long moment. Finally, the one on the left nodded. Breathing a sigh of relief, she slipped out the door, letting it close softly behind her. She was unsure which way to go, so she decided to wing it. She settled on right and headed down the hall. Relieved, she found her way to the top of the stairs, the same way Malcolm had brought her. All she had to do now was get out of the castle and to the copse of trees. She hoped like hell the time bender was still there.

So far, she made it sight unseen. But she didn't think that would last long. She heard voices drifting up to her. She knew the outside of the castle would be heavily guarded. She paused on the stairway, straining to listen. Thick Scottish brogue lilted to her ears. She pressed against the cold stone wall on the stairs and peered around the corner into the great hall to watch and listen.

The man who entered could only be Robert Bruce, his booted feet resonating off the stone walls. He was a tall man with soulful brown eyes and a full head of thick dark hair. He looked lean and muscular, much like a warrior of his time should look. He wore a thick fur cloak around his shoulders and shrugged it off as he entered, then dropped it on the bench next to him.

He was accompanied by Campbell and another man Skye assumed was a Scottish laird of importance. Why else would he travel with Robert Bruce? He was a head taller than Robert with a sword at his side wearing a tartan in the same colors and pattern as Malcolm, boots and a fur cloak.

"Thank ye, brother, for bringing Robert to us." Malcolm and his brother clasped hands and arms in a brotherly greeting.

Skye eyed him, noting the family resemblance between the two. Both handsome. Both tall and muscular. Both with long plaits in their hair.

"William and I rode hard to get here. What news of Alanna?" Robert said. Campbell offered Robert a tankard of ale, but he waved it away. "Did ye find her?"

Skye's gaze flew to William as she stared hard. William was Malcolm's brother. Malcolm's last name was Wallace. This was William... *Wallace*? Her heart did a weird ka-thunk in her chest as she looked at the historical legend before her. The man who led the resistance to the English occupation of his beloved Scotland. He had big, powerful hands, thick forearms and was a wall of muscle. The size of that sword hanging at his side was...enormous. She'd read somewhere that the guy was tall. Something like six-foot-five. And he looked it. All two-hundred-and-whatever pounds of him.

For some reason, all she could think about was that Mel Gibson movie *Braveheart* and she wondered how much of that was based in fact. Probably not a lot since Hollywood tended to take creative license for the sake of drama instead of historical accuracy.

She couldn't help it. She gaped at him.

"Aye, we did." Malcolm gave a nod, his face grim.

"Is she all right, then? Where is she?"

Campbell and Malcolm exchanged a glance before Malcolm continued. "The news is no' good. I'm afraid she was murdered."

"By English scum no doubt." William punctuated his words with hot spit hitting the stone floor.

"Murdered?" Anger flashed in Robert's brown eyes, and he pounded his fist on the table. "By whom? Do ye ken?"

"We dinna ken yet." Even as Robert roared, Malcolm remained calm. "But we suspect she was killed by English soldiers. I believe Edward had no intention of the marriage taking place, Robert."

"It would appear so," Robert replied, his jaw muscles flexing. "I must make my apologies to the family."

"Ye should wait. 'Tis likely what Longshanks wants. To lure you out," William said.

"Aye," Malcolm agreed. "And there is another situation to deal with."

"And that is?" Robert pinned with him his gaze.

"'Tis another girl who looks much like Alanna," Campbell said. "Malcolm found her and brought her here."

Skye stifled her gasp with her hand at her mouth. Crickey. They were talking about her now. What grand scheme were they going to concoct?

"Aye? Go on." Robert was intrigued.

"We think ye should marry her under the guise she *is* Alanna," Malcolm said. "And we can prove then to Edward ye held up your end of the terms."

Anger fumed through her. How dare they marry her off like she was some piece of property. She didn't even *belong* here, much less should she marry Robert the Bruce. She may not remember everything about her history class, but she knew for a fact he *did not* marry a noble woman to gain Scottish independence. They fought a long, bloody battle for it.

"Thereby turning over the rule of Scotland to me," Robert finished.

"Aye," Malcolm and Campbell said in unison.

"With ye marrying the girl, he will surely have to abide by his own promise," William said. "'Twould be the perfect plan."

Robert gave a nod of agreement. "It is a grievous circumstance, to be sure, but a good plan that has come of it. I will advise the nobles at once what has transpired."

"No, dinna do that," William said.

"Why not?"

"It could be one of them betrayed you. Only we and the nobles knew of the plan to marry you and Alanna and now Alanna is dead," William said.

Malcolm nodded agreement. "Aye. We should keep this between us only."

"Then we continue the ruse, as if she were the real Alanna?"

"Aye. No one kens but a few of us here that she is dead." Malcolm picked up a mug of ale and took a swig. "And only a few of us saw the other girl."

"Has she agreed to this? Who is she anyway?"

"She appeared last night in the trees. She seems to have no kin," Campbell said.

"Then it should be easy to convince her," Robert said.

Fury scalded through her as they decided her fate, talking about her as though she was nothing more than a bargaining chip. A pawn in an elaborate political game that had nothing to do with her. As though her life was not her own. She was a twenty-first century woman. She was an American. She was not going to allow them to do this to her.

She stepped out of the shadows and hurried down the remaining steps. She paused at the bottom with her hands fisted at her side.

"You're not going to convince me of anything," Skye said. Even to her own ears, she sounded like a spoiled brat, but she didn't care.

All eyes turned to her. She tried not to falter under the scrutiny of four medieval men staring her down.

Robert looked her up and down. "I take it this is your lassie then, Malcolm?" he remarked at length, smiling wryly. Malcolm nodded. "Aye. She'll do."

Skye didn't like the way he looked at her. He was prettier than the others at the table, clearly marking him as a noble who had never set foot on a battlefield. She could tell the others had seen their days of war and knew they would continue to see them.

"The resemblance is remarkable," Robert continued. "She's as lovely as the real Alanna."

"Stop talking about me like I'm not here." It was all she could do to keep her emotions in check. Wasn't it enough that she was in a strange place? She really didn't need these male chauvinists planning her future.

Malcolm rose, came around the table for her, fire in his blue eyes. She suddenly felt like a child in his presence and cowered. He snatched her by the arm. "Ye best mind your mouth, lassie."

"Or what?"

She had to crane her neck to glare up at him. She wasn't afraid of the towering man, even though she scarcely stood as tall as his shoulder. She *wouldn't* be afraid. She was driven by her need to get the time bender back safely in her possession.

Robert stood then and stepped in front of her. He fingered her coppery hair framing her face and gazed at her with a look she didn't like at all. She slapped his hand away.

"Don't touch me."

Never mind that Malcolm still clutched her arm in his hand. She didn't mind that so much. However, she did mind being handled as if she was precious property. Of course, after overhearing their conversation, it appeared she would be. What they would do with her *if* she married Robert Bruce worried her the most.

"Malcolm, perhaps ye should explain to the lassie what is going to happen to her if she doesna cooperate," Robert suggested. "For now, I take my leave."

And then he was gone, leaving Malcolm clasping Skye's arm and Campbell to stare after him. William, still seated, chuckled.

"She's got a fire in her belly, that's for sure," William said. "Where did ye say ye found her?"

"It doesna matter. Come, lassie."

Malcolm dragged her outside into the crisp night air. She gulped in deep breaths as if it were the last chance she had for freedom.

"You can't keep me here," she protested. "I need to go home. I need to find..."

She broke off. She couldn't tell him about the time bender or that she was from the future. He'd never believe her. Malcolm came to a halt and turned to her, putting his hands on her shoulders and looking deep into her eyes. It gave her a jolt and her breath caught in her throat.

"We need yer help, lassie." His voice was soft and not at all edgy like she expected. "Did ye hear what we talked about?"

"Yes, but I can't help you."

"Ye mean ye won't help." He dropped his hands to his side, looking defeated.

"No, it's not that." She sighed, wondering if she should even bother to tell him the truth. "You wouldn't believe me if I told you and I haven't the vaguest idea where to begin. I'm not from here."

"*Och*, aye, I ken that. I can tell by the way ye talk." He folded his massive forearms over his chest. "The others ken, too, but it doesna matter to Robert."

She sighed, her breath pluming in a white cloud as she gazed up at the night sky with a million stars blazing bright against the inky blackness. It was so different from her night sky. She'd lived in the city all her life where street lamps washed out the stars and she could only see the brightest ones on the clearest night. Here, she could see every pinprick of light. Even the Milky Way. It was astounding.

But gazing at all those stars until she died—if she stayed—didn't make her want to be a part of this world. Even if she *was* to marry a Scottish legend. How could she make him understand? The truth was, she couldn't.

"Tell me who ye are, lassie. I willna be angry."

"Oh, it's not that I'm afraid you'll be angry. It's just that...well...it's complicated. I can't help you because it would change—" She stopped, unsure of her words.

Who was Skye Ransom to alter history? She wondered what would happen should she marry Robert under the guise of this murdered woman, Alanna. Would Edward Longshanks relinquish control of Scotland? She doubted it. He was hell-bent on keeping Scotland under English rule.

"Change?" he prompted.

"I'm from a different place," she tried.

"Aye, so ye said. I'm no' blind. I can see," he said.

Glancing up at him, she saw in the half-light he grinned. It was infectious and she smiled back.

"Yes, well, you have no idea how different."

She paused, searching for something to say, some reason he'd let her leave the castle and return to the woods. As she stood there, staring up at his face he suddenly seemed so trustworthy, and she thought perhaps there was a chance he could become her ally and help her find the time bender. After all, what better person from whom to enlist help? He would know the woods in the dark like the back of his hand.

"Tell me, then, lassie..." He paused, staring at her with a look she couldn't read. "What is yer name?"

"My name?"

He took a step closer. "Aye, yer name."

"I'm..." She halted, unsure. Should she tell him her real name?

"Yer...?"

"Skye."

"Skye?" He tipped his head in question. "Yer named after the heavens?"

She giggled. "Yes. Where I come from it's a beautiful name."

"Somebody's coming!"

Malcolm started to reply when he was interrupted by the shout at the gate. He jogged over to see who arrived and Skye followed. It was a group of men, more Scotsman, and they entered the castle grounds carrying a man on what looked like a crude, make-shift stretcher. She inched closer so she could hear what they said.

"Found him on the hillside," said one. "Surrounded by the English."

"He claims he's no' one of them," another chimed in. "'Tis strange to me to be seein' a man on a hillside with the English, though."

"Are ye English?" Malcolm asked the man on the stretcher.

His head rolled from side to side.

"Ye are no Scotsman," Malcolm said, giving him a close once-over. "Who are ye then?"

"If I told you the truth, you would never believe me."

The voice was unmistakable. The dialect was American. Modern. *Dane.* Skye shoved her way through the gathering men and stopped short. Her eyes widened.

She couldn't believe it. His gaze met hers, surprise flickering in the depths.

"You," she gasped. "You really *are* here."

# Chapter Nine
## A Promise

CHAPTER NINE: A PROMISE

Skye whispered the words, her breath crystalizing in front of her. She moved to stand beside the make-shift stretcher. He still wore his muddied and torn twenty-first century clothes and looked like he'd taken a beating.

"Are you..." He started to reach for her, but someone pulled a sword and pointed it in his face. He dropped his hand. "What happened?"

Moving seemed to hurt him, and he twisted and grimaced. Beads of sweat formed on his forehead.

Malcolm, surprised by their mutual knowledge of each other, looked to Skye, his brows raised inquisitively. "Ye know each other, lassie?"

"We do."

So, this was what had become her father's bodyguard. When he fell into her in the dressing room, he'd traveled back in time with her. Somehow, they had become separated along the journey. The ride through time had ripped them apart and he wound up somewhere else in the woods nearby.

"Who are ye then?" Malcolm demanded.

"Just a traveler in a strange land," Dane said, his piercing green eyes pinning Skye.

"Malcolm, he has a broken leg, I think," one of the men said then.

"Take him inside. I'll fetch the healer then." Malcolm hooked his thumb toward the castle behind them.

Skye watched them take Dane away. She couldn't believe it. He was here. He had actually made it back in time with her. Now, at least, she had an ally. Someone who would understand what she was going through. She was no longer alone.

A thought thundered through her. Maybe he had somehow ended up with the time bender and they could get out of here before the Scotsmen married her off.

"How do ye ken this stranger?" Malcolm asked.

"Uh..." She shifted from one foot to the other. "It's a long story."

Because how could she tell him that Dane Fortune was hired by her father to protect her? Maybe her father had some foresight that put Dane in her life for this very reason. Maybe he was supposed to travel back in time with her.

She shoved away the thoughts. It was silly to think her father would know what would happen to her. He couldn't determine the future any more than she could. Dane's appearance in her life was a classic right place/right time instance and one for which she was grateful. If he hadn't picked her up in that car, she may have ended up dead.

"Is he dangerous?" Malcolm continued to watch the men heading away from them.

She didn't truly know the answer to that question. She knew Dane for all of fifteen minutes and had no idea who he really was, deep down. All she did know was he'd been hired by her father, and he'd tried to protect her from the hit man. He could be the most lethal man in the world, for all she knew.

Even so, she shook her head. "I don't think you have to worry about him. Where are they taking him?"

"To one of the bedchambers. I best find the healer."

But he made no move to leave. Instead, he turned and looked at her, a contemplative on his face.

"What?" she asked, folding her arms over her chest.

"You will help us, won't ye, Skye?"

She looked up at him, met his gaze. His face was etched with concern, worry, hope. And all of that was riding on her. But how could she possibly agree to marry Robert Bruce when she knew it was historically inaccurate? She'd alter history for all time. What would be the repercussions of that? What would happen to England if Scotland won its independence simply by an arranged marriage?

She had another more immediate dilemma. She needed to get her hands on that time bender. With her mind racing, she came up with a story she hoped would sound plausible enough to convince *him* to help *her*. She exhaled a breath she hadn't known she held.

"When you found me in the woods, I dropped something. It was a...a pendant...sort of...about this long, silver." She demonstrated by spacing her forefinger and thumb apart, approximating the length of the time bender. "It was a gift from my father. He was killed and it's all I have left of him. I...I need to get it back."

Malcolm's brows drew together in question. "What does this have to do with helping us?"

She took another deep breath. "If you let me look for it...then...I'll help you."

He gave a quick shake of his head. "I canna be letting ye go."

She blinked, staring up at him. "Why?"

"No' unless ye promise first to help me."

He'd caged her in, leaving her no choice. She had to agree so she could get back out to those woods and find the time bender. She shifted from one foot to another, her stomach in a tight knot. She was about to reply when he took her chin in his hand and tipped her face up to his.

"If this pendant means that much to ye...then I'll help ye find it."

"You will?"

"Aye, I will."

She couldn't stop the flood of relief that went through her. In her moment of sheer joy, she hugged him.

"Thank you, Malcolm. Thank you so much."

He pulled away from the embrace to give her a broad grin. "'Tis fine, lassie. I'll see about our patient."

She fell in step beside him as they walked away. She knew she should feel guilty for lying to him, coercing him into helping her especially after he'd been so kind. Still, it was something she couldn't help. She had to get away from there.

She thought of Dane then. "I need to see him."

He gave her a sideways glance. "Who is he to ye?"

"A friend," she said.

He gave a nod and motioned for her to follow him. Relief went through her. She'd talk to Dane and figure out a way out of this mess. They had to get out of there before they were stuck there forever.

# Chapter Ten
## Uneasy Reunion

THE MEN PUT DANE in a bedchamber with nothing more than a narrow bed with a feather mattress and a couple of crumpled pillows. He knew he had a sprained ankle. It hurt to move it. He'd experience a lot of pain in the past—he'd been shot, stabbed, beaten—but there was something horrible about being stuck in a medieval world without the ability to walk. Their medicine practices were primitive at best, and he doubted he'd be running any marathons anytime soon.

His back ached, his leg throbbed, his head screamed in agony. His landing had been less than ideal. He wiggled his fingers to test them and found, thankfully, they weren't in pain. But his right elbow stung and, strangely, his ass hurt. His shirt was dirty and the sleeve was torn. His pants were covered in grass stains.

He thought long and hard about his circumstances. His long, bumpy and oh-so-painful journey to the castle had given him plenty of free time. He knew it wasn't some stage show. They weren't actors. It was real. All of it.

And Skye was here. She'd used the time bender, either on purpose or by accident. What he didn't know was what happened to the hit man, Archimedes Crane. Or Ark as he preferred.

Dane knew him. Not personally, but he knew him. He'd seen enough intel on the guy to know who he was and that he was bad news. The former Navy SEAL had gone rogue and turned into a hired gun to take out some of the most high-profile and high-ranking officials in government and the military. Of course, there was no proof he was responsible, but Dane suspected.

For Conner Dade to hire him, he had to have some serious cash. Dane heard through his connections the hit man was in for one last big job before he retired. He had no idea he, himself, would be involved.

The really scary thing was once Ark was hired to do a job, he wouldn't stop. Even if they made it back to their time, Ark would continue to hunt Skye until she was dead. He had the Terminator mentality with lethal skills.

Dane had no doubt he was the one who was responsible for the death of William and Emily Ransom.

It was no wonder why Conner Dade wanted the time bender. With it, he could alter the past, mold the future. He could go anywhere, do anything. With William's research notes and journals in his hands—if he indeed was the one who stole them—there would be no way to stop him. Then where would that leave him and Skye? Trapped? Or would Conner figure out a way to come after them in the past?

The other thing that concerned him was Ransom's missing notes and journals. Thomas hadn't made a big deal over those, assuming Conner had stolen them, but Dane wasn't born yesterday. He'd been around long enough to know with DARPA and the NSA involved, there had to be some other dark forces at play.

He didn't even want to go there.

At any rate, Dane would do whatever it took to keep Skye alive and out of danger. He needed to talk to her and soon. He remembered Thomas's warning about the unpredictable time bender. He wasn't scared of a lot of things, but being trapped in the past with no way to get home definitely topped the list.

He heard voices outside his door. He knew they stood guard while trying to decide what to do with him. As if they needed to. He wasn't going anywhere with his bum ankle. If it was any other time under any other circumstance, he could take it easy with his ankle. However, time was of the essence, and he needed to find Skye. And maybe some whiskey to dull the pain.

The door opened and the tall man addressed as Malcolm entered. He was followed by another Scotsman who shut the door. As Malcolm stood, arms crossed over burly chest, the second man approached the bed. He watched as the man he assumed to be the healer ripped open his pants to examine his leg. As the healer ran his hand down his leg then over his ankle, Dane winced and flinched.

"I'm no' sure the leg is broken, but the ankle is no' looking good," the healer said. He nodded to the swelling of his left ankle. It had already started to bruise, too.

Internally, Dane rolled his eyes. He knew what was wrong with his ankle, but he couldn't tell this Neanderthal that. He needed to ice it down but that was impossible here.

"Can it be managed, Angus?" Malcolm asked.

"I dinna ken."

"Bind it with a bandage," Dane said. "That will keep me from injuring it further. And I need to elevate it."

The two of them looked at him as though he'd grown a second head. Dane reached for the pillows behind him and tucked one under his foot, giving it a little elevation.

"Like that."

"Are ye a healer, then?" Angus asked.

"Not exactly but I've had this type of injury before."

"I'll fetch a bandage, then."

Angus rose and shuffled from the room, leaving Malcolm to tower over Dane. The burly Scotsman fixed Dane with a scorching glare of suspicion.

"The woman says yer no' dangerous."

"I'm not," he was quick to say. "We know each other. We're...friends." It wasn't exactly the truth, but it was close enough. The truth was he hardly knew that girl except from the very little William Ransom told him. And that wasn't much at all.

Malcolm nodded. "'Tis what she said, too. She wishes to see ye."

"And I need to see her. Talk to her."

He hummed a response before turning to the door. He pulled it open. Skye rushed inside still wearing that ridiculous gown from the costume shop. He could see the lumpy outline of her street clothes under it and nearly chuckled. Except he noticed then her pretty features were etched with concern as she approached. Dane was relieved to see her and sensitive to the way she looked at him. She was worried about him.

"I'll leave ye be, then." Malcolm left and closed the door behind him.

Skye waited until they were alone to breathe out a sigh of relief. "Dane, thank God. I'm so glad you're here."

"Where's the device?" he asked, getting right to the point.

Annoyance replaced relief as it flashed over her face before she got it in check. "I think I dropped it when I landed."

Fear pounded through him. "You *dropped* it?"

"I landed in the woods. I haven't been able to leave to look for it."

"Skye, how the hell are we supposed to get out of here without it?"

"Hey, don't snap at me. I didn't know I'd dropped it until it was too late. It was an accident."

"And was using the damn thing an accident, too?" He practically growled the words. He knew he was being an asshole, but he couldn't stop himself.

She huffed and folded her arms over her chest, pushing her breasts up and together. He could see the hint of a little cleavage at the top of her gown, and he berated himself for looking.

"You fell into me in the dressing room, remember? So, yeah, I *accidentally* pressed the button. Maybe you could stop being such a jerk about it and help me figure this out."

He ran his hand over his face. He had to remember she was young—a college girl—and he had at least ten years on her. She was basically still a kid, and he was a well-seasoned former military man. She didn't deserve his wrath. It wasn't entirely her fault she sent them back in time.

"Sorry, Skye. I'm just cranky and in a lot of pain."

Her gaze flickered over his bruised and swollen ankle. "Is it broken?"

"No. Just a bad sprain. I'll be all right."

She chewed on her lower lip. "How did it happen?"

"After I woke up, I tried to get my bearings. I twisted it."

She winced and flushed, her cheeks turning a pale shade of pink. "Does it hurt much?"

"I'll live. The healer went after a bandage to bind it." He leaned his head back against the remaining mound of pillows and stared up at the ceiling, trying not to look at her. He'd been in worse shape and had always managed to pull through. "So, what's your plan to find the device?"

"Well, I..." She hesitated, paced the length of the room. "I made a deal with Malcolm. He's going to help me look for it."

Dane didn't like the sound of that. His head snapped up as he looked at her. "What sort of deal, Skye?"

She waved it away. "It doesn't matter right now. Do you have any idea where we landed? What time period?"

He would have shrugged if he could. "In the past, obviously, but I don't know the year."

She moved closer to the bed and dropped her voice. "It's during the time of William Wallace. He's *here*, right now, in this castle. Malcolm is his brother."

Dane searched his memory banks for the threads of history he could recall. He was no historian, but he knew they'd managed to land in the middle of a tumultuous time in history. The Middle Ages were barbaric, and it was really no place for a lady.

"That would be during, what, the thirteenth century? Scotland is at war with England trying to win its independence."

She nodded vigorously. "Yes. As soon as I can get out of here, I'm going to search for the time bender with Malcolm."

He narrowed his gaze at her. "Can you trust him?"

She didn't answer right away as she met his gaze, her indigo eyes full of concern, question and wariness. He understood, then.

"Can I trust *you*?" she asked.

They looked at each other for a long, quiet moment. He lowered his voice, making sure he sounded as confident and sincere as he could. "With your life, yes. Always."

A breath shuddered out of her. He moved on, quickly, so she'd stop looking at him like that.

"You said you made a deal with Malcolm. What was it?"

She swallowed hard and paced again. "I...promised to marry Robert Bruce."

Dane stared at her hard trying to decide if that was a good idea or not. He was leaning toward *not* as she rushed on.

"I realize it will alter the future—"

"You can't do it, Skye."

"I know but it was the only way I could get Malcolm to help me. I had to agree."

"Well, un-agree. You can't go through with it."

"I can't take it back. And anyway, how can I get out to search for the thing without help?"

"I'd help you, but..." He waved to his ankle.

"No, you can't. You need to get better. We don't have much time left before we can use the time bender again. Thomas said seventy-two hours, right?"

Dane nodded. "What's your plan?"

"I'll get Malcolm to take me out to the woods so I can look for it. As soon as we can, we make the jump to get back home."

She sounded so confident, he hated to burst her bubble. He clearly remembered Thomas telling them they may not be able to get back to where they started. And there was something else about alternate realities. He didn't want to voice his worries yet until there was a reason.

"Be careful."

"I'll be fine," she said.

A knock on the door preceded it opening. The healer had returned with what looked like a handful of rags and Malcolm hot on his heels.

"Come with me, lass, so the healer can do his work."

Skye pinpointed Dane with a questioning glance. Even if he didn't like the Scotsman, Dane gave her a nod.

"Go. Come back when you find it."

She gave a quick acknowledgement, then turned to Malcolm, wrapping her arm around his. "Let's go."

# Chapter Eleven
## Castle Attack!

"Find 'it'?" Malcolm asked after they were alone in the hall.

She smiled, trying her best to come up with a good answer. "He doesn't know what he's saying. He's in a lot of pain."

A deep groan came from the other side of the door. She knew that was Dane. She grabbed Malcolm by the hand.

"Let's go to the woods to search for my pendant."

He lifted an eyebrow. "Now?"

"You promised to help me." The sooner they hit the forest, the sooner she could find the time bender. She hoped.

She dragged him toward the winding stairs. Malcolm went willingly but she sensed a bit of hesitation. Even so, she pushed on to get him out of the castle. As they exited the stairs and headed through the great hall, William intercepted them.

"There ye are, Malcolm." His gaze flickered over her. "Where are ye taking her?"

"I lost something in the woods," she said.

William shot her a glare before directing his gaze back to his brother. She got it. Women and children should be seen, not heard. She clenched her jaw.

"'Tis time to discuss Stirling," William said to his brother.

The Battle of Stirling Bridge. Skye pressed her lips together so she wouldn't say it aloud. While she didn't recall the outcome, she knew the famous battle.

Malcolm turned to her with an apologetic look on his face. "Sorry, lass. I canna go with ye now."

"But—"

He released from her grasp and headed off with William, leaving her alone. She watched them go and knew what she had to do. She had to search without him. She didn't need a chaperone. She marched toward the great castle entrance and slipped out without being noticed. Once in the bailey, she glanced around to get her bearings. The cold air hit her in the face, and she shivered.

The curtainwall was nearly twenty feet high with a walkway guarded by men stationed at every gatehouse. The guards kept a watchful eye on all those coming and going. No one was getting in or out without some-one knowing about it. Men trained with swords and other primitive weapons. Makeshift tents had popped up all around the bailey. Horses were led into and out of the nearby stable. Men were squabbling over who got the right to stay in the building that housed the knights.

Crap. She'd never get past them.

Several men noticed her and stopped to gawk. She clutched her elbows as heat rushed to her cheeks. This was a mistake.

One warrior approached her and looked her over. He was young but scruffy-looking with dirt on his face, neck and hands. He held a sword in one hand at his side.

"Are ye lost, lass?"

"I was...um..."

"Ye're Alanna, aren't ye?" he asked. "Ye belong to the Bruce."

She stiffened. Yes, of course, that was the angle she needed to take. "Aye, I am. And I am going for a walk." She motioned to the gate.

Another man joined the first. "A walk? Ye canna be going out there alone."

"I am perfectly able to take care of myself." She sounded as haughty and forceful as possible.

"We canna let you go alone, lass," the first man said.

"No, we canna. So, Gavin will go with ye." The second man clapped Gavin on the shoulder with a bright smile. Then he gave him a nudge, like he was getting a prize.

Annoyance flashed through Skye. She was no one's prize. But she also knew they'd never let her out without an escort. She gave a nod of agreement.

They headed toward the gate. Gavin explained the situation to the men guarding it and they allowed them passage. But as they headed out, someone called Gavin. He stopped, turned and waved, then addressed her.

"Wait here," he ordered.

As soon as his back was turned, she curtsied to the guards and made a break for it. They were so stunned, they couldn't react fast enough. She clutched her skirt in her fists to keep from tripping over it as she ran as hard and fast as she could. Behind her, she heard shouts, but she didn't dare turn around. She only stopped when she made it to the edge of the trees and disappeared within them. She paused to catch her breath before making her way through the dense foliage.

It was tough to get through the maze of undergrowth in the dress she wore. It kept catching on the branches around her and she had to stop and detangle herself. When it caught again and ripped, she'd had enough.

She pulled the dress off over her head and tossed it in the underbrush. Skye breathed a sigh of relief to be in her street clothes at last.

She stood for a moment, trying to remember where William had picked her up. Had she come to over there or somewhere else? She'd never find the time bender in this place. With her hands on her hips, she scanned the area and saw the log she remembered from earlier. That was where Malcolm found her. That was where she woke up.

Skye hurried over and fell to her knees. The underbrush was thick here. She shoved aside wet leaves and bracken in a frantic search for the time bender.

She came up empty handed. Her heart sank. What if a wild animal carried it off? What if some unsuspecting Scot picked it up and took it? She'd never find it again. She and Dane would be stuck there forever.

Hot tears burned the backs of her eyes as she sat there, blinking them back and trying not to break down into wracking sobs. She'd lost so much. How much more would she lose? She was in the past with a man she barely knew. Her parents were dead. Her college days were officially over if she couldn't get back. She'd have to find some way to live in this primitive world.

She threw herself a spectacular pity party surrounded by nature listening to the sounds of the birds singing...and the pounding of horses' hooves.

Yes, definitely horses.

She got to her feet and crashed through the woods to the edge of the trees and then halted. Several men on horseback approached. Whoever they were, the men on the castle walls didn't like the looks of them and closed the gates before the intruders could get there. Arrows rained down on them, while the others fired back from horseback.

A rumbling caught her attention and that's when she saw the battering ram crash into the gate. The thick wood shuddered with every hit, but nothing was getting through it or those thick castle walls.

At least, that's what she hoped.

Skye crouched down, her heart in her throat, as she watched the attack on the castle unfold. Were they English? She didn't know because she didn't know enough about history. All she did know was she was stuck outside, alone and scared and worried about Dane, William, Malcolm and the others.

What was she going to do?

All she could do was hide in the underbrush, shivering, until it was safe to return.

When the healer arrived with a handful of crude bandages, Dane waved him off. He didn't need or want his help. Angus watched with rapt interest as Dane went about wrapping his ankle with the longest bandage and then securing the ends with a tight knot. When he was done, the man gave a nod of acknowledgement and then left.

He was relieved it was only a sprain and not something worse, like a break. He shuddered to think what they'd do for a broken leg in this place. Remembering his head wound, he reached up again and touched it. His head was sore, for sure, but the wound had clotted, and it didn't seem to be a very deep gash. He had been lucky.

They both had. Skye looked uninjured.

Next time they might not be so lucky.

Dane, though, had to find a way to walk out of there. He wasn't a cripple, but the injured ankle would certainly slow him down. He swung his legs off the bed and tested the bad ankle. Yeah, it hurt like a sonofabitch but the binding seemed to help. He could at least keep upright. Taking a step hurt, but maybe he could muscle through it. The worst thing for the ankle would be to not use it.

He stared at the door, wondering if he had a chance, if he could get out of this hellish, barren room with a very uncomfortable bed——if it could even be called a bed. More like a medieval torture device.

Dane hobbled to the door favoring his injury and reached for the archaic handle. With his hand on the lever, he paused, listening. But he heard nothing through the oak door. That could be a good thing or bad.

He lifted the lever and slowly opened the door with a creak. Peeking out, he saw the corridor deserted. Not one Scottish guard stood outside his door. Perhaps they thought since he was laid up, he would be rendered immobile.

He heard shouting down the corridor and down the stairs. He made his way to one of the arrow slits down the drafty hallway to peer out. There were men rushing about along the curtainwall. Arrows flew and a thundering sound came from one of the gates.

Battering ram?

He hobbled to the top of the stairs and peered down the tight spiral with doubt pressing the back of his mind. The stairs were too steep and too narrow. He didn't think he could make it down the stairs with his injury. How was he going to get to Skye to make sure she as all right? It wasn't like there was an elevator in this place.

He had to go for it. He took the first step with his left foot. Knowing he would have to put weight on it, he cringed. There was no handrail, so he didn't have anything for leverage. He had to take that first step, but the pain was so intense, he broke into a hot sweat. A wave of sickness shifted through him. He backed away from the stairs and sagged against the cold stone wall.

That's where one of the Scottish warriors found him. He gave him a questioning look.

"Help me down the stairs?" Dane asked.

"Ye're the stranger," the man said. "The one brought on the stretcher."

"I am. I'm trying to find my friend. The woman."

"I dinna ken where she is."

Dane pointed down the stairs. "Down there." With that man. That very handsome Scottish laird. "I need someone to lean on while I make it down the stairs."

The man gave him a nod. "All right then. I'll help ye."

DANE HOBBLED HIS WAY out of the castle and into the bailey where the pounding of the north gate was loud and intense. The scene was chaos. In all his years in the military, he had never seen anything like the medieval warfare going on right in front of him.

Men ran through the bailey, arming themselves and taking up a spot on the curtain wall. Arrows rained down over the wall to the intruders while return arrows made their way over the wall and pierced the ground as well as hitting a few of the Scottish defenders.

He had to do something. He couldn't stand there and watch men die. But there wasn't a lot he could do with his injury.

The gate door splintered and cracked as the battering ram made its way inside. The intruders poured in. Dane spotted Malcolm and another man similar in looks and stature defend the castle. They fought back with swords, killing everyone their blade came in contact with.

It was a gruesome scene.

If Malcolm was here, then where was Skye? He scanned the battle scene, looking for her fiery hair but didn't see her. He hoped she was inside the castle and not out here. The men attacking the castle didn't seem to be like the English soldiers he'd encountered on the way here. No. These seemed like Scotsmen, too. Why would they fight each other?

The only thing Dane knew to do was take up arms and fight against them, too.

And that's exactly what he did. He took the sword and shield of one of the fallen.

Favoring his injured ankle, he fought his way to Malcolm's side. Together, they killed man after man. Malcolm gave him an appreciative nod as they fought side by side. Even William seemed as though he approved of his fighting tactics.

Dane wasn't sure he was using the sword correctly. All he knew he was when he swung it, it hit his intended target and did damage. He took a few hits, but ultimately, he came out splattered with blood but unscathed.

When the last of the intruders were dead, Malcolm and William surveyed the carnage.

"Where's the messenger boy? We need to send a message to MacLeod his coup failed." William punctuated his words with hot spit next to one of the dead men. Then he stomped off to find the messenger boy still clutching his bloodied sword and looking as though he'd been to a massacre.

"Who were they?" Dane asked Malcolm.

"The MacLeods are a warring clan from the Highlands. They believe Robert Bruce has no claim and are trying to put their own noble laird on the throne." He, too, spit next to the dead man. "This was Hamish MacLeod. Eldest son of the clan leader. Now dead."

Before Dane could reply, a man hurried over to Malcolm. "Where's the fire-haired girl, Alanna?"

"She's no' in the castle?" Malcolm thumbed over his shoulder.

The man shook his head. "She left before the attack."

"What do you mean she left? Left where?" Dane asked. Panic flickered through him.

"Gavin was supposed to escort her on her walk," the man said. "He was called back and returned. She ran through the gate. We tried to stop her..."

"*Och.* God's teeth, woman," he swore under his breath. "I ken where she could be. I'll get her." He turned to Dane then. "Stay here. Yer in no shape to be following me."

"But—"

"Nay. Stay. I canna carry ye both back."

He charged off through the destroyed gate, snatching a torch on his way out, leaving Dane no choice but to remain behind.

# Chapter Twelve
## Deception and Lies

Skye had lost track of time. The cold seeped into her bones. She found her discarded dress and tugged it back on, trying to keep warm. Then she found that fallen log, sat against it and drew up her knees. She huddled there in the cold and the mist and listened to the sounds of battle.

Her head dropped down to her knees, her breath pluming in and out as she listened and worried and tried not to cry. She hated everything about this place. All she wanted to do was go home and she couldn't even do that because she couldn't find the damn time bender.

She would be married off to a Scottish noble and then she'd die here.

She drifted off with her head still on her knees, trying her best not to shiver when all she wanted to do was shiver. She heard a distant voice shouting. It sounded like her name. She lifted her head and was shocked to see night had fallen.

She'd been out there since morning?

Her stomach rumbled something fierce. Her legs and arms were stiff from sitting on the cold ground.

"Skye! Where are ye, lass?"

Yes, she for sure heard that. And he was near. It sounded like Malcolm. She pushed to her feet. "I'm here!"

He came crashing through the trees carrying a torch, his tartan wrapped around him to ward off the chilly night air. Orange-yellow light flickered over his face, illuminating the worry lines.

Relief flooded through her at the sight of him and she sank to sit on the log. A spurt of hot tears sprang to her eyes. She couldn't control them even if she wanted to.

"What the devil are ye doing out here? God's teeth, woman! Ye gave me a fright."

"I-I came looking..." Her teeth chattered so hard, she couldn't finish.

"Bollocks. Ye came looking for that pendant alone? *Och*. Ye could have been killed."

As he neared, she could see blood splattered across the front of his tartan. He carried his blood-stained sword in his other hand. Her gaze flew to his face. She could see spots of dried blood along his neck and face.

"Wh-what happened?"

"Opposing clan tried to invade." He spat on the ground with disgust. "We held them off, though." He sheathed his sword and held out his free hand. "Come, lass. Let's get ye inside out of the cold."

"But my pendant..."

"No, Skye. Ye'll catch yer death."

He took off his tartan and wrapped it around her shoulders. It was still warm from his body heat. It seeped into her from head to toe. She could even feel her cheeks warm from the small gesture.

"We'll have to search for it in the morn. Now come." His tone indicated he wanted no argument.

Relenting, she took his hand. His big, warm hand. He pulled her to her feet with a quick jerk. She stumbled into him, landing against his wall of muscle. He smelled of sweat and blood and something more masculine than any man she'd gotten close to in her limited experience. He wasn't like the boys of her time. He was one-hundred-percent alpha male.

His arm wrapped around her to steady her and suddenly she wasn't cold anymore. Their eyes met. Her heart stopped, then kicked into overdrive. The only sound was that of the flickering torch and her suddenly labored breathing.

They looked at each other for a long moment and then it happened. He kissed her.

His warm mouth landed on hers in a solid, sweet kiss that literally took her breath away and stole her senses. It was nothing more than a brush of the lips, really, before he realized what he'd done and quickly pulled back.

"I shouldna have done that." He broke their embrace and took her by the hand. "We should get back. Robert will be looking for ye."

"Oh," was all she could say.

He was right. Robert the Bruce would want to know if his imposter bride was all right. Would Dane be worried about her, too? As he led her from the log, she caught a glimpse of something shiny sparkling in the firelight. Her breath caught in her throat as she gasped. She jerked her hand free and fell to her knees, shoving leaves out of the way.

There, on the ground, was the time bender. The heady sensation of relief pounded through her.

"I found it!"

She snatched it, held it up in the torchlight so she could get a better look at it. Thankfully, it still looked as though it was intact. The tiny screen was dark, but she hoped that was because it was off and not busted.

Malcolm snatched it out of her hand before she realized what happened. "This is the pendant ye were so worried about?"

"Hey! Give that back. It's mine."

"No' so fast, wee one."

There was a strange glint in his eye as he held the time bender out of reach. She jumped, her hand grasping for his but it was no use. She merely caught air and nothing more. A sick feeling crept over her and her stomach plummeted to her knees.

"But...what...are you doing?" she asked.

He tucked it into his sporran, which happened to be right in front of his groin. Clenching her fists, her fingernails dug into her palms. Was this a game? Did he expect her to go after it? Her anger flared, making her see spots. And then red. And any minute now she was going to explode.

"I'll give it to ye *after* ye wed Robert."

Fear clawed its way to her throat. Oh, crap. She was actually going to have to go through with it?

"You can't be serious."

"I am. 'Tis mine until you wed. Do ye no see, lassie? We canna fight the English forever."

She nodded slowly. "No, you can't."

She couldn't argue with him. He had it and she wasn't going after it. At least she'd found the thing and there was some hope of getting back home. She could tell Dane and maybe he'd have a plan for getting it back from Malcolm and getting out of there before she was married off.

Skye held up her hands in surrender. "You win."

He smiled with triumph. "Good, lass. 'Tis the right decision ye made." He started to go, then turned back to her. "Ye willna tell Robert about—"

She waved it away. She had no intention of telling anyone about the kiss. "No, of course not."

With that, he led her back to the castle. But she would never forget the way his mouth felt against hers. Never.

As they approached the castle, Skye could see the ground littered with dead outside. A smoldering fire was inside the bailey, and she could tell it was what was left of the battering ram that smashed through the gate. More dead were inside the bailey. The ground was a mixture of blood and mud. The air was tinged with death, charred wood and scorched tar.

Skye walked behind him as they entered the great hall. The men were all in high spirits after their victory. A feast had been prepared with all sorts of roasted meats including whole boar and venison, numerous loaves of bread, a wheel of cheese, a platter with leeks and potatoes in a creamy sauce, a bowl of apples and oranges. The ale and wine flowed. Laughter rattled the rafters. And there sitting at one of the long tables, was Robert Bruce and William Wallace.

The sight was surreal to Skye. Her damp hair was still plastered against her head. She pulled the tartan tighter around her and clutched her elbows. The girly side of her wished she didn't like something the dog dragged inside after a rainstorm.

"Mayhap we should get ye cleaned up." Malcolm took her by the elbow and led her back up the stairs. "Ye look a fright."

"Gee, thanks."

She knew she looked like hell. She'd been outside all day in the cold freezing her ass off during the battle. In a way, she was glad she had been gone so she didn't have to experience the horrors of war.

"I'll have a washtub brought up for ye." He looked her over with a critical eye. "And mayhap a new gown."

She glanced down at the wreck of a dress she had on and nodded. The skirt was torn and dirty. "Yes, I think that'd be nice."

As the paused at her room, she slipped off his tartan and handed it back to him. Their hands brushed and she wished he was the one she had to marry, not Robert Bruce.

"Go on then. I'll wait for ye outside and then we'll go down together."

He closed the door behind him, leaving her with a warm tingling sensation. Oh, how she wished she could do something about the amorous feelings bubbling inside her.

When he left her alone, she wondered where Dane was. She hadn't seen him in the great hall, but then again, he was injured so likely he was still in his own room.

A knock and a moment later, three female servants entered with a steaming pot of water and a copper wash basin. One of them had a pile of dresses and dropped them on the bed. The very idea of three strange women seeing her wet and naked set her teeth on edge.

"I prefer to bathe alone," she announced.

It garnered her shocked looks by all three of them.

"You two go on. I'll help the lass." The older of the three shooed them out of the room and closed the door. She turned back to Skye, her hands on her hips. "Now let's get ye clean."

DANE'S ANKLE ACHED SOMETHING fierce. But he'd made it to the great hall post-battle and sat against one of the walls with his foot propped up on the bench beside him. He was content to sit alone and watch the festivities while he worried about Skye's well-being.

When he discovered she was missing, he knew there was no way he could go after her himself. Letting Malcolm go alone was the only option. However, he had not expected her to come back with him looking flushed and happy and wrapped in his tartan. It annoyed Dane.

He knew it had nothing to do with the fact he couldn't keep her safe. It had everything to do with the way she looked at the Scot.

What had happened out there?

It enraged him even more Malcolm took her upstairs to the bed chambers and hadn't returned anytime soon. Even more unnerving was neither one of them saw him brooding in the corner alone.

Just as well. He didn't need pity.

Sometime later, he spotted William Wallace approaching from the other side of the great hall. He stiffened and sat a little straighter. The man was a legend. Dane had done is best to steer clear of him during the battle. He didn't know what interacting with the man would do to the historical timeline, so he preferred to err on the side of caution, unlike Skye. The man perched on the bench across from him, leaned heavily on the table and peered at him with intense blue eyes.

"Ye fought well out there, stranger. What do ye call yerself?"

"My name is Dane," he said. "I know who you are."

He nodded, as though he knew his reputation preceded him. "My brother tells me ye are a traveler from a distant land."

"I am." And he'd really like to get back to that distant land. He hoped Skye managed to reacquire the time bender.

"We could use good men like ye," William continued. "Brave men who are willing to fight. What say ye?"

Dane blinked, staring at him. Was William Wallace asking him to join their cause? He almost laughed. There was no way he could do that. What if he died before he'd even been born?

"I see the hesitation in yer eyes," the man continued. "There was no hesitation when ye killed those men earlier. Why now?"

No, there wasn't. He knew a hundred ways to kill a man with a knife or a gun, but he'd never used a sword and a shield before. It was definitely a first for him and something he wouldn't soon forget. Even so, it was not his preferred method of warfare. How could he explain? He took a deep breath and tried.

"I know what King Edward has done to your country. It is a great injustice. I know you'll fight hard for any victories and those will be well-deserved. The Scottish are a resilient, determined people. I have every confidence you'll—"

Dane halted when he caught a glimpse of Skye entering the great hall on Malcolm's arm. His mouth went bone dry. Her copper hair had been washed, brushed and wound about her head in the latest fashion. She wore an azure gown that did wonders for her skin tone and her unusual lavender colored eyes. Quite simply, she was stunning.

He didn't miss her deer-in-headlights look, though. She was terrified.

William followed his gaze to her. "*Och.* Nothing but trouble there for ye, laddie. She belongs to Robert Bruce."

He knew the deal. He clamped him mouth shut and tore his gaze away from her. "I know."

He turned back to Dane. "Are ye willing to join us or no'?"

If Skye could play along, then so could he. If he said no, then the chances of them sending him away grew. If he stayed, then he could stick around when Skye married Robert to make sure she was all right. And then they could get out of there together.

He met William's gaze and gave him a nod. "I will."

"Good then." He rose and headed back to his previous seat next to Robert.

Malcolm positioned Skye so she was seated on Robert's other side, then sat across from them. She caught Dane's gaze and gave him a little nod of acknowledgement.

"After today's attack, it is clear to me we must accelerate plans for the wedding. Once wed, we can avoid the fight at Stirling Bridge altogether and prove to Longshanks once and for all we have held up our end of the agreement," Robert said. "William, when does the priest arrive?"

"Should be here within a fortnight."

"That's not soon enough." Robert shook his head. "We need someone to marry us as soon as possible. Find a priest."

"Your pardon, my lord," Skye interjected. All eyes went to her. Color stained high in her cheeks as she fluttered her lashes at the noble. "But mayhap a handfasting would suffice?"

They stared at her, mute, for long seconds. Finally, Robert nodded. "That could work. It would signal our intent to marry officially in the church, thereby fulfilling the deal made with King Edward." He addressed William then. "Find handfasting cords or ribbon. Anything will do. We marry in the morn. After we consummate, we will then make our way to York to prove our union to the king."

William gave a nod and rose, leaving the great hall to fulfill his request. Robert turned to Skye then, took her hand in his and kissed the back of it gently.

"A brilliant idea, lassie. Together, we will make a powerful couple. I canna wait to marry ye."

Dane clenched his hand into a tight fist. He couldn't allow this sham of a marriage to happen, no matter what the outcome was. He needed to get her alone and find out if she'd managed to get the time bender back. They needed to formulate a plan. They needed to get out of there.

A breath shuddered out of her as she glanced Dane's way, her eyes wide with horror. She quickly recovered as she looked back at Robert.

"I look forward to it, too, my lord."

"I'll escort you to your chamber so you may rest."

Dane remained in place, a slow simmer of annoyance and anger boiling under the surface, as he watched the two of them walk away.

# Chapter Thirteen
## Plans for Escape

CHAPTER THIRTEEN: Plans for Escape

A ball of regret and terror clumped in the middle of Skye's stomach. She knew suggesting the handfasting would be a risk, but it was one she was willing to take. Until Robert announced to God and everyone he intended to consummate their marriage before leaving for York.

Good Lord. What had she gotten herself into?

She tried not to think of it and not allow the terror to overtake her as the Scottish nobleman escorted her from the great hall to her bedchamber. Like Scarlett O'Hara, she'd think about that tomorrow.

He paused at her door and turned to her, taking both her hands in his. "I look forward to our marriage, Alanna."

Her mouth was dry as the Sahara. She forced the lie through her lips. "As do I."

"Your name really isn't Alanna, is it?"

She shook her head. "No, my lord."

"What is it? Will you tell me?"

She bit her lip. The last thing she wanted to do was tell him her real name. Malcolm knew and that was enough for her. "Does it matter? I'd much prefer you call me by her name to continue the ruse."

A smile tugged at the corner of his mouth. "As you wish."

He cupped her cheeks and tipped her head back and suddenly her heart whammed against her chest. Oh, God. He was going to kiss her. She stiffened as he leaned into her and their lips touched, brushing ever so softly against hers. It was a completely different kiss than Malcolm's.

"Til the morn." He released her and turned to go.

She sagged against her door and watched him walk away. She'd lost her mind. How in the bloody hell was she going to get out of this handfasting ceremony and get the time bender back?

Again, she'd think about that tomorrow.

She pushed open her chamber door and plopped down on the feather mattress, staring up at the ceiling as she chewed on her lower lip. It was hard not to feel utterly hopeless, not to let it consume her when all she wanted to do was let it.

As she brooded, a knock sounded on her door. Her heart did double time as she sat up and stared at it. Another knock. This time more urgent. She hopped off the bed and hurried to it opening the door to see Dane standing on the other side.

Without waiting for an invitation, he shoved his way into her room and closed the door, staring at her with a look that said he was none too pleased with her.

"What the hell were you thinking?"

She folded her arms over her chest and gave him her best glare. "I was thinking the sooner we get on with this wedding, the sooner we can get out of here. I found the time bender."

He didn't react. In fact, he kept his face completely impassive. "Well? Where is it?"

"Malcolm took it from me. He has it. And I can't get it back until I marry Robert Bruce." The calamity of the situation hit her hard. She ran her fingers down her face and turned away as fear jangled her nerves.

Silence descended between them. Dane shuffled to the bed and perched on the edge. "All right. That's all right. We can figure this out."

"How?" she whined. "I've screwed everything up."

"No, you haven't. We just have to figure out how to get the time bender from Malcolm without you consummating that marriage."

"Good luck with that." She sounded sour even to her own ears.

"At least you found it," he said. The relief was evident in his voice.

She looked at him over her shoulder. "I did. I don't know if it still works, though."

"We'll worry about that when the time comes. Right now, our priority is to get it back and get someplace where we can use it."

She heaved a sigh as she paced the room. If she could somehow get close to Malcolm, maybe she could get her hands on the time bender before the wedding. She halted suddenly as a plan came to mind. She knew Malcolm was interested in her. They'd kissed after all. Maybe she could use that to her advantage. She bit her thumbnail.

"I have an idea." She looked Dane's way. "But you're probably not going to like it."

He narrowed his eyes. "What is it?"

"Malcolm...likes me. I think I can use that to our advantage and get back the time bender."

"You mean sleep with him?"

"No!" Blood pulsed to her cheeks, and she knew she blushed. "I was thinking more like flirting."

He scowled. "Are you sure that's a good idea?"

Of course, it wasn't, but it was all she had. "Yes. I can do this." She charged to the door.

"Skye, wait." She halted, turned to look at him. "Be careful."

"I'll be fine." She pulled open the door and went in search of Malcolm.

As she headed down the hallway, it occurred to her that it probably wasn't the best plan. She was treading on thin ice with Malcolm, but she was sure she could get back the time bender. She found her way back down to the great hall. If anyone asked her what she was up to, she'd tell them she was looking for something to eat. What she found was a moping Malcolm sitting alone at one of the long tables with a tankard of ale in one hand.

She halted. Their eyes met. His went from dull to shiny and bright. He sat a little straighter.

"Lassie, what are ye doing down here? Ye should be resting for yer day."

"I couldn't sleep." It was the truth. She'd never fall asleep in this place with the wedding to Robert the Bruce looming. "You couldn't either, I see."

He shoved away the tankard and got to his feet, staggering a little as he did so. That was good. She'd have his drunkenness in her favor at least.

"Go to bed, lass."

He stumbled toward her, no doubt intending to head to his own bed. She stepped in front of him, looking up at him with adoration in her eyes. Her heart went into overdrive and her mouth went bone dry.

"What if I didn't marry Robert? Then what?"

He peered down at her, question in his blue eyes. "What are ye saying, lass? That ye dinna want to marry him? It could put our alliance with England at jeopardy."

"That's just it. There is no alliance with England. It's nothing but a farce." The moment the words escaped her, she knew she'd said too much. She pressed her lips together to keep from spilling any more about history. A history she really knew nothing about.

"Ye canna back out now. Ye gave me yer word."

She wrung her hands, trying to decide how best to proceed. "I know...it's just that I..."

She looked up at him again, fluttered her lashes. And then she took a deep breath and flung herself into his arms. He had no choice but to catch her. She wrapped her arms around him and pressed her lips against his. He tasted like ale and the undertones of smoked meat. And while they kissed, she slipped her hand into his sporran. Her fingers fumbled in the small pouch until she brushed the cool metal of the time bender. Her hand closed around it, and she pulled it out, slipping it into her dress pocket.

Mission accomplished.

Malcolm came to his senses long enough to shove her away. His lips were glossy from kissing and his eyes were wide and red-rimmed.

"Ye shouldna have done that."

"I-I'm sorry. I thought we had a connection. I thought—"

"Yer promised to Robert. My feelings for you dinna matter, lassie."

His voice was soft but firm. It sent a tingling sensation through her as she took a step back. She pressed a hand against her the butterflies fluttering in her stomach. He had feelings for her? What had she done? All she wanted was the time bender. She got that. She could go home now, but something bothered her. Malcolm would likely die in battle. In the short time she'd gotten to know him, she'd grown attached to him. In her own time, he was nothing but a ghost. But here, in his time, he was flesh and blood. A lump formed in her throat. She swallowed it hard.

"You know as well as I do this wedding is nothing but a charade."

He turned away from her. His shoulders slumped. "Go to bed, lassie."

With her heart in her throat, she fled back through the castle, up the stairs and to her room. When she made it to her door, she sagged against it. She could not explain the hot tears stinging her eyes.

"Did you get it?"

Dane's voice behind her startled her. She yelped and spun to face him, her heart doing a wicked tattoo.

"You scared the life out of me."

"Sorry." At least he had the good sense to look sheepish. "Are you all right? You look flushed."

"I'm fine." She said it through clenched teeth as she pulled the time bender out of her pocket and thrust it at him. "Here."

"You got it. Good." He turned it over in his hand, looking at it with a critical eye. "How does it work?"

She glanced up and down the hallway. "I don't think we should talk about it out here."

Nodding, he clutched it in his fist. "Right. In here." He motioned toward her door.

Back inside her room, she flung herself on the bed and put her arm over her eyes. Why couldn't he take the thing and leave her be? Not that she wanted to stay here. She wanted to go back home, yet she couldn't stop the overwhelming sadness enveloping her.

"What's wrong with you?"

"Nothing. I'm tired is all."

"Tell me how this thing works." There was an insistent edge to his voice. She wanted to fling sharp objects at his head.

"Press the black button."

There was a pause then, "Nothing happened."

Skye huffed. "Thomas said it wouldn't work for seventy-two hours. How long have we been here?"

"Maybe not long enough. Wait. I can see something on the screen. Faint numbers it looks like."

That got her attention. She sat up, then reached for it and snatched it from his hand. Faint green numbers were on the screen.

"It's not much but it is something."

Her finger hovered over the button as she met his gaze. He gave her a nod of encouragement. She pressed the button.

Nothing happened.

She pressed it again.

Still nothing.

"Maybe we have a few more hours to go," he suggested. "We'll try again in the morning." He shuffled to the door favoring his injured ankle.

But all she could think about was in the morning she'd be wed.

# Chapter Fourteen
## Bride on the Run

SKYE WOKE TO SOMEONE banging on her door. It took her a few moments to realize where she was as she cracked opened her eyes. Her head pounded right along with whoever was pounding on her door.

"Lass, open the door," Malcolm called.

She'd slept with the time bender clutched in her hand all night long. As the door opened, she righted herself and shoved it deep into the pocket of her gown. Malcolm charged in, his eyes wild. He still wore the blood-stained tartan and clutched a sword in one hand.

"What it is?"

"The English are coming. We must wed ye at once to Robert. Come quickly." He waved her toward him.

"But—"

"No time, lass."

She glanced down at the rumpled gown she wore, dismayed she didn't get a chance to change. Not that it mattered. It was still a sham of a wedding, and she was nothing more than an imposter. She slid off the bed and took his hand.

They hurried down the stairs to the great hall. William Wallace, Robert Bruce and a few of the other clansmen waited. She didn't see Dane. Sudden worry gnawed at her. As soon as they came into the great hall, he released her hand.

"We must hurry," Robert said without bothering with a greeting. He seemed not to notice Malcolm holding her hand. "The English are crawling the countryside. The handfasting must proceed as quickly as possible. Let's make haste to the chapel."

He and the others preceded them out of the castle. But Skye hesitated. She had never been married. Hell, she'd never had a serious boyfriend. This was life altering and it certainly wasn't the wedding of her dreams.

"Come on, lassie." Malcolm took her by the arm.

Once they were outside, they hurried toward the chapel. Despite the circumstances, she was ready to get this over with so she could go home. When they entered, Robert and William were waiting, including Campbell and Dane. Relief sputtered through her at the sight of her only ally.

"Come, Skye." Robert held his hand out to her.

She hesitated again. She thought of the time bender in her pocket. She wondered if it would work and if she could transport herself home, even if that meant leaving Dane behind. She glanced his direction. His brows knit as if he sensed her sudden betrayal.

"'Twill be fine, lassie," Malcolm said softly. "Go now."

She slipped her hand from his arm and reached for Robert Bruce. With her hand in his, she knew it was the first step to changing history and changing her life forever.

William Wallace stood at the head of the altar, ready to preside over the ceremony. He held four ribbons and waited for them to present their interlaced hands to him. Robert took her hand in his, extending their twinned fingers toward the warrior.

"We're ready now," Robert said with a nod. "Make haste."

"Alanna and Robert, I bid ye look into each other's eyes and answer faithfully. Will ye honor and respect each other and seek to never break that honor?"

"We will," Robert said.

When she didn't answer, he gave her a look of encouragement. She cleared her throat. "We will," she said, her voice faint and scratchy.

William draped the first ribbon over their hands. "And so, the first binding is made. Will ye share each other's pain and seek to ease it?"

"We will," they said in unison. And a little piece of Skye died.

William draped the second ribbon over their hands. "And so, the second binding is made. Will ye share the burdens of each, so that yer souls may grow in this union?"

Her heart pounded harder as they both answered. William draped the third ribbon over their hands.

"And so, the third binding is made."

As he spoke, outside there was a sound of something whistling through the air and then a loud crash. The chapel walls shuddered on their foundation.

"Trebuchet!" someone shouted.

"Hurry, William," Robert said.

"Will ye share with each other all the days of yer life, in sickness and health, until death unto ye part?"

Her mouth felt as though it was full of cotton, but she managed to get the words out. William draped the fourth ribbon over their hands and quickly tied them together.

"As yer hands are bound together, so are yer lives and souls joined in a union of love, devotion and trust."

"We're under attack!" another voice shouted.

"Let no man put ye asunder. I pronounce ye handfasted as man and wife."

Robert gave her a shove toward one of his men. "Protect her with your life," he said, then to the others, "Come!"

"What? No kiss?" Skye muttered. "Some husband you are."

Skye stumbled into the arms of a stranger. She quickly pushed away, straightening her dress. She whirled to see Malcolm and the others dash from the chapel. Only Dane remained. He hobbled to her as quickly as his sore ankle would allow him. He grasped her arm, tugging her away from Robert's man left to stand guard over her.

"Now's the time," he said, his voice low. "Let's go."

"I want to tell Malcolm good-bye."

"Skye, don't be foolish," he urged. "We have to go *now*."

"I'm not leaving without seeing him. End of story."

There was another crash into the side of the chapel, rumbling its walls. Dane grasped her by the arm. "Let's get out of here. Use the time bender, Skye, before we're killed."

She pulled it out of her pocket and opened her fingers, looking down at it in her hand. The LCD green read-out showing the date looked odd. She held it up closer to examine it. The date reading looked warped, with parts of the digital numbers missing. The same as last night.

"The numbers showing the date are still faded." She held it up so he could see.

"We have to give it a try anyway."

She was about to answer when Malcolm burst into the chapel. He ran to her, grasped her by the hand.

"Ye must get out of here." He dragged her toward the door. "'Tis no' safe here."

"I'm coming with you." Dane limped after them.

"Malcolm, wait," she said, trying to stop.

But Malcolm ignored her pleas and headed away from the chapel and out of the gatehouse. She could hear the yells and screams of the men and smelled blood on the air. She heard the clash of swords and the sound of boulders crashing into the castle launched from the trebuchet. Malcolm dragged her away from the destruction and battle and into the trees. She glanced over her shoulder to see Dane hobbling after them, hurrying as best as he could with his hurt ankle. Malcolm paused in the woods, held her by the shoulders.

"Ye must go now, lassie," he said.

"What about Robert and going to York?"

"Dinna fash. I'll handle him. I ken ye are no' from here, lassie."

"I'm not," she admitted. "I'm—"

"Shh." He pressed two fingers against her lips to silence her. "It doesna matter. All that matters is ye get to safety."

Those hot tears were back.

"Yer pendant—"

"I have it." She opened her hand to show him. "I took it back last night."

He smiled. "Clever girl."

Suddenly faced with the reality of leaving, she quaked with fear. She hugged him, feeling her cheek press against his damp tunic. "I don't want to leave you."

"Ye must," he said softly. He pulled her away, cupped her chin in his big hand and tipped her head back. "Just as I must face the battle before me. I bid ye farewell now, lassie."

He leaned down and kissed her, his lips barely brushing hers. But she wasn't going to let him go so easily. She fisted his tunic, pulled him to her, and kissed him hard, passionately, taking even her own breath away. When at last she released him, he stepped back, his blue eyes full of wonder.

"I really wanted that this time," she whispered. "I'll miss you, Malcolm."

Then Dane crashed onto the scene, panting and sweating. He wiped his brow with the back of his hand.

"I hope you've said your good-byes, Skye," he panted. "Because there are Englishmen headed our way." He limped to her side and hooked his arm in hers. "Let's go."

Holding her breath, she looked at Malcolm. She wished there was time to explain to him, to make him understand, because she could see his eyes were suddenly filled with confusion. *I'm sorry, Malcolm,* she thought and pushed the button.

THE WORLD AROUND HER seemed to disappear and she fell into a black abyss. She felt Dane's arm was still linked with hers and then...nothing. He was gone, out of her grasp. She could neither see nor feel him in her descent into nothingness.

She felt as though she was ripped apart, limb by limb. She opened her mouth to scream, yet no sound came out. She couldn't breathe. It was as though the wind was knocked out of her. Nothing like the previous experience when there was simply nothing at all. Had she blacked out sooner last time? She couldn't recall. Then there was a heavy pressure on her chest, crushing her, stealing the life from her. Mercifully, she blacked out.

When she regained consciousness, she felt cold and numb. Even her bones were icy, achy, as though she lay on a sheet of ice. She opened her eyes to blinding whiteness. Lifting her head, she realized the white surrounded her as far as she could see. Bright red spread underneath her and she was horrified to find she was in a pool of her own blood.

She sat up and screamed.

# Epilogue
## Scotland, 1297

THE SKIRMISH HAD ENDED, leaving the castle in ruins. But the English invading force was defeated, leaving behind numerous dead on both sides of the battle. Malcolm and his brother along with Robert Bruce and Campbell made it through it alive.

As things settled, Robert found Malcolm, who had already decided he would perpetrate the lie that would alter their battle plans yet again.

"Where is my bride? Is she safe?"

Malcolm clutched the pommel of his sword, his palm slick with blood and sweat. "She's dead, my lord. Captured and murdered by the English."

Rage colored Robert's features. "I wish to see her body at once."

"My lord—"

"*Now*," Robert insisted.

Malcolm did not miss the look of surprise on Campbell's face. He ignored him and waved for Robert to follow him. They hadn't buried the dead girl yet. No. Instead they put her body in the crypt while they decided how to proceed once Bruce, and the imposter girl made their way to York.

Campbell caught up with Malcolm and spoke low in his ear. "What are ye about, Malcolm? Where's the girl?"

"Gone. Left with the stranger."

It was all he was willing to say. He could not explain the wild lightning storm that surrounded them as the girl named after the heavens held the small silver pendant. Mayhap that was how she got her name.

"This canna be the way—" Campbell started.

"'Tis the only way," Malcolm said.

At the crypt, Malcolm prayed Robert would not notice the girl—the real Alanna—had been dead for some time. The noble looked upon her pale face that resembled the woman he'd handfasted only hours ago. The bruising on her neck had not faded much, either, lending credibility to the story she had been brutally murdered.

Robert looked her over. First sadness for the loss of the girl and then anger colored his face.

"Longshanks men. She was found in the woods after the battle," Malcolm said as they all looked on.

There was a long moment of silence and then at last the man history knew as Robert the Bruce spoke.

"I shall avenge her. William, I want ye to sack York and then lead the battle at Stirling Bridge."

Without another word, Robert the Bruce left the crypt. The tides had turned. Scotland would continue to fight.

As for Malcolm Wallace, he would remember the woman named Skye until the day he died.

# Next in the Series
## Dead of Winter

**At the mercy of a faulty time machine, will Skye and Dane be able to make it home alive?**

At the mercy of a faulty time machine, Skye Ransom and Dane Fortune are forced to randomly leap through time on a wild, roller-coaster ride of danger as they try to get back to the 21st century. Each jump sends them farther away from home, but brings them closer together in a bond that not even a time bender can sever.

With their last time leap, they end up in a strange futuristic frigid world with two opposing tribes. The arrival of the time travelers sets into motion a long-dead prophecy indicating Skye is the future of one of the tribes, causing a rebellion. When one of the tribe leader's kidnaps Skye intent on marrying her, and sacrificing her to the gods to help him win that rebellion, Dane uses his military tactics to launch an all-out war to save her before she's burned alive on a funeral pyre. But will he be able to save her before it's too late?

# Also by Michelle Miles

**Age of Wizards (Epic Fantasy)**
In the Tower of the Wizard King
On the Hunt for the Wizard King

**Dragon Protectors (Paranormal Shifter Romance)**
Desiring the Dragon Lord
Seducing the Dragon Knight
Tempting Her Dragon Bodyguard
Dragon Protectors Book Collection (Books 1-3)

**Dream Walker (Urban Fantasy)**
Call of the Dark
Blood and Bone
Flame and Fury
Smoke and Ashes
Light of the World
Dream Walker Collection (Books 1-5)

**Enchanted Realms (YA Fantasy Romance)**
Once Upon an Ancient Curse (Newsletter Subscribers Only)
Once Upon a Midnight Clear
Once Upon True Love's Kiss

Once Upon an Enchanted Kiss

**Five Towers (YA Fantasy Romance)**
The Sorcerer's Daughter

**Ransom & Fortune Adventures
(Time Travel Action/Adventure)**
Highland Fling, Vol 1
Dead of Winter, Vol 2
The Citadel, Vol 3
Lord of the Underworld, Vol 4

**Realm of Honor (Fantasy Romance)**
One Knight Only
Only for a Knight
A Knight to Remember
A Knight Like No Other
Shadows of the Knight
Realm of Honor Collection (Books 1-5)

**Guardians of Atlantis (Fantasy Romance)**
Tempting Eden
Seducing Eve
Ravishing Helene
Guardians of Atlantis Box Set

**Shorts and Anthologies (Fantasy/Paranormal)**
*Newsletter Subscribers Only*
A Dance Among the Faeries, Short Story
Eorwulf, Short Story

The Soul of Sharah, Short Story
Flights of Fantasy: A Collection of Short Stories
Dragons of Emhain Short Story Collection


*Watch for more at MichelleMiles.net*

# About the Author

MICHELLE MILES believes in fairy tales, true love, and magic. She writes fantasy (including Epic, Urban, and Other Worlds), Paranormal (including Time Travel, Historical, Shifters), and Young Adult (including Fantasy and Fairy Tales) all with an action/adventure twist. She is the author of numerous series that includes everything from angels and demons to fairies, dragons, and elves.

She is a member of Romance Writers of America (RWA) and Science Fiction and Fantasy Writers Association (SFWA). A native Texan, in her spare time she loves reading, listening to music, watching movies, hiking, and drinking wine. She can be found online at Facebook, Instagram, Pinterest, and more!

**Magical Worlds, Daring Adventures, Unforgettable Romance!**

*Read more at MichelleMiles.net*